FOREVER, PLUS ONE

(THE INN AT SUNSET HARBOR—BOOK 6)

SOPHIE LOVE

ISBN: 978-1-64029-108-9

BOOKS BY SOPHIE LOVE

THE INN AT SUNSET HARBOR
FOR NOW AND FOREVER (Book #1)
FOREVER AND FOR ALWAYS (Book #2)
FOREVER, WITH YOU (Book #3)
IF ONLY FOREVER (Book #4)
FOREVER AND A DAY (Book #5)
FOREVER, PLUS ONE (Book #6)
FOR YOU, FOREVER (Book #7)

THE ROMANCE CHRONICLES
LOVE LIKE THIS (Book #1)
LOVE LIKE THAT (Book #2)

CHAPTER ONE

The noises of the bustling yacht club seemed to fade into silence as Emily heard her own voice repeating the words she'd just spoken.

"I'm pregnant."

Opposite her, Daniel and Chantelle wore twin expressions of surprise. Neither uttered a word. Emily herself felt too stunned to say anything else. It had only been a minute or so since the pregnancy test she'd taken in the yacht club restroom had revealed her new reality. It hadn't properly sunk in yet.

It was Chantelle who finally broke the silence. Not with words, but with a squeal of delight. Her joyful exclamation seemed to shake Daniel from his trance. He reached across the table and grabbed Emily's hand tightly. Tears sparkled in his eyes.

"Really?"

Eyes locked on Daniel, Emily nodded. A wave of emotions rushed at her. It wasn't just shock now, but excitement, delight, joy. There was a baby growing inside of her! She was having her own child! She and Daniel had created a new life together. Their love and commitment had brought them this moment of blissful wonder.

Chantelle started bouncing up and down in her seat. "I'm going to be a big sister!" she cried.

Emily and Daniel's intense moment dissipated as they were brought back to the here and now by Chantelle's exuberance. They both laughed and Emily nodded in affirmation of her statement.

"When will the baby be born?" Chantelle asked eagerly.

Emily shrugged, still struggling to accept her new reality. "I don't know yet."

She counted back in her head, trying to work out when she could have conceived. The baby, though wanted, was not planned. A happy accident had happened somewhere along the line.

Emily thought about the funny turns she'd been having recently, the ones she'd put down to stress, and the numerous moments of nausea that she'd assumed were anxiety. Could they have actually been the first signs of pregnancy? She'd been so rushed off her feet recently—what with the wedding, the adoption, her father, and Roman Westbrook—that she hadn't even realized her period was late. As she thought about it now she realized that she'd last had one the week before they married. Weeks ago. If she'd conceived on their honeymoon, she may already be halfway through her first trimester!

"We'll have to speak to the doctor," Emily explained to Chantelle. "They'll be able to work out how long I've been pregnant and tell me the due date."

"It will still be lots of months," Daniel added. "So you'll have to be patient."

Patient looked like the last thing Chantelle would be able to be.

"Can we make a calendar?" she asked, her eyes wide and sparkling. "So we can count down the days?"

Emily beamed, touched by Chantelle's enthusiasm. "That sounds lovely," she said.

"Can we make it really big?" Chantelle continued. "As big as a whole wall?" She stretched her arms out as far as they could go.

Emily nodded. "Okay!"

"With rainbow colors?"

"If you want!"

"And glitter?"

Emily laughed. "That sounds wonderful."

It was such a relief for her to know that Chantelle was happy for her. Sheila's pregnancy had caused a whole host of emotions to erupt in Chantelle, compounded by the fact that her friend from school, Toby, was also soon to become a big brother. Emily had been slightly concerned that Chantelle may act out as a result of the news. But so far she seemed nothing but excited. Emily reminded herself to let her teacher, Miss Glass, and Gail, the school counselor, know about the situation in case Chantelle had a delayed negative reaction to the news.

Daniel's expression turned serious for a moment. "Chantelle, will you be able not to tell anyone about this yet?" he asked.

She looked at him and frowned, visibly deflating like a popped balloon. "Why not?"

Emily knew why Daniel wanted to keep it hush for now. She wasn't yet past the critical first trimester. This was her first pregnancy and she was an older mother. At thirty-six it fell into the horribly titled bracket of a "geriatric pregnancy." The chances of her miscarrying were higher than average. The thought caused a jolt of alarm to shock her.

"So we can keep it our special Morey family secret," Emily said, tapping her nose. "It will make it more fun."

Daniel looked up, his expression relaxing somewhat, presumably at the way Emily was handling the slightly delicate situation.

Chantelle's frown turned to suspicion. Then it disappeared as quickly as it had come.

"Okay!" she said, raising her eyebrows, suddenly on board. "But then, what about Papa Roy? He's family but he's a Mitchell, not a Morey."

Emily considered her question for a moment. What about her father? Should she tell him before the first trimester was over? Should she tell anyone? She'd need emotional support, that was for sure. She just didn't know who would be best placed to give it to her. Her father had only just come back into her life, after all. She didn't know how well he'd handle adjusting to being a father, father-in-law, and grandfather in one fell swoop!

"Maybe a bit later," she told Chantelle. "For now, let's just have it be between us three. Okay?"

Chantelle mimed zipping her lips. Everyone laughed.

Across the table, Daniel reached for Emily's hand again. He squeezed it tight, his eyes gazing at her adoringly, and mouthed the words, "I love you."

Emily smiled to herself and mouthed them back. This moment was so perfect, so beautiful. She felt blessed that her life had finally aligned so perfectly.

*

That night, Emily and Daniel lay together in bed.

"I can't sleep," Emily confessed, rolling onto her side to gaze at him.

Beneath the covers she felt Daniel's hand move protectively over her stomach.

"I wonder why," he said with a chuckle.

Emily rested her own hand on top of his. "I know, I can't quite believe it's real. Maybe once I've seen a doctor, had an ultrasound, I'll believe it."

"An ultrasound," Daniel repeated with awe. "I never got a chance to do any of that stuff with Chantelle."

Emily felt sorry for him. Daniel had missed out on so much of Chantelle's early life, including her birth. Things were going to be so different this time around. He'd get to experience every moment of their baby's life, all the firsts; first smile, first sneeze, first step. The thought warmed her.

"So when will we get to see our baby?" Daniel asked. "When's the first ultrasound?"

"Twelve weeks, I think," Emily said, realizing that she herself didn't know a huge amount about what was going on. Her pregnancy was something they would have to learn about together. "I'll know how far along I am once I see the doctor."

"Do you think you conceived on our honeymoon?" Daniel asked.

"I hope so," Emily replied with a grin, remembering their lovemaking in vivid detail, knowing that the time they'd spent together on their honeymoon would never be forgotten.

Daniel fell quiet then. "What shall we do about telling people? Friends. Staff." Then more quietly, he added, "Moms."

Emily sighed. She'd been ruminating on it also. Neither of their mothers were in their lives in any real capacity. Both were difficult personalities, both had failed their children in the past. They would likely fail at being grandmothers, too. If they couldn't put their issues aside in order to witness their children's marriage, what hope was there for them playing any kind of active role in their grandchildren's lives?

"Let's not think about them just yet," Emily said. "I want to stay happy for at least a few weeks. Can we do that?"

Daniel nodded and turned his face toward the ceiling. Emily thought he seemed a little subdued, reserved. She hoped it was just over the mother issue and nothing more. But she couldn't help worrying that there may be something else. Perhaps the news of the pregnancy wasn't entirely welcome for Daniel. He'd wanted to plan their child together, after all. Maybe he was disappointed that it had just been sprung on them?

Emily decided against prodding him for an explanation. Daniel, she hoped, would come to her in his own time to share whatever concerns he had. It wasn't like she herself wasn't filled with anxiety over her ability to parent, or over the child's health, the future, even the state of the world it was soon to be born into! There were a million things to worry about now. It would take some time for them both to process it.

She snuggled down beneath the covers, her mind still running on overdrive, imagining what the future might hold. A son or daughter? Blond hair like Chantelle, or dark like her own? What would they call it? What room should they use as the nursery? There were so many things to think about.

She took a deep breath, trying to calm herself. Best to take things one step at a time. The first thing to do was get an appointment with the ob-gyn.

CHAPTER TWO

Emily felt as nervous as a child on her first day at school as she sat on the bed in the obstetrician's office, swinging her legs beneath her. Daniel looked just as much out of his depth as he sat in the hard plastic seat beside her. There were framed medical certificates on the mint green walls, colorful posters showing the different phases of pregnancy, and the unpleasant smell of antiseptic lingering in the air. Emily realized she was going to have to get used to this environment. Over the next few months, she'd be smelling a whole lot of antiseptic!

The door swung open and in walked the doctor, Rose Arkwright. On first impressions, Emily thought she was dressed very smartly, more like an attorney than a doctor. It was really only the comfortably flat shoes, the white doctor coat, and the stethoscope around her neck that gave her away.

She smiled at them both as she placed her clipboard down beside her computer and took a seat at the desk.

"Mr. and Mrs. Morey?" she asked, addressing them both. "Firstly, may I say congratulations."

She had a warm smile, Emily noted, and she shook each of their hands with a firm, confident grip. Emily got the distinct impression that Doctor Arkwright was an intelligent, no-nonsense kind of person. She felt like she was in very safe hands.

"Thank you," Daniel said, smiling shyly. "We're over the moon."

Emily was glad to hear him say as such. She wasn't entirely sure how he felt since he'd seemed a mixture of shocked and stressed yesterday.

"Shall we get right to it?" Doctor Arkwright said. She flipped over the first piece of paper and looked at Emily. "I'm afraid I'm going to have to take a lot of detailed notes to begin with. Forms, forms, and more forms."

"No problem," Emily said. "Fire away."

"The first thing we need to determine of course is how far along you are. Are your periods usually regular?"

Emily nodded. "My last one was just before our wedding. So it's been about eight weeks."

"So this might be a honeymoon baby?" Doctor Arkwright said with a smile. "How romantic."

Emily blushed.

Doctor Arkwright continued. "The way we work out the due date is to initially take it to be thirty-eighty to forty-two weeks after the end of the last period. So currently we're looking at December eleventh."

Emily and Daniel looked at each other, their eyes wide. So close to Christmas!

"Then when you have your first sonogram and the baby is measured that can be adjusted slightly," the doctor added. "Can you tell me what symptoms of pregnancy you've been having and how long for?"

"She was feeling nauseous and faint," Daniel explained. "From right after the wedding really, wasn't it?" He looked over at Emily for confirmation.

"I thought it was stress," she said. "There was a lot going on in our lives at that point of time."

Doctor Arkwright nodded. "They're the two most common symptoms to have early on. And often confused with stress. No fainting, though? Just feeling woozy?"

"Yes," Emily said.

Doctor Arkwright took notes as she spoke. "Good. It's not dangerous to the baby if you do faint because it's too small at the moment and in a protective sac of fluid. But for you it can obviously be a bit distressing, particularly if you hit something on the way down. Keep an eye on that going forward. It's likely to resolve over the next few weeks but for some women the symptoms do persist. If you're naturally prone to low blood pressure it could continue into the second trimester. So make sure you take it easy. Stand up slowly. Eat regularly. Best to keep a banana in your purse. And a bag of nuts."

"Sure thing," Emily said, nodding, already starting to feel a little overwhelmed. She wished she was taking notes and hoped Daniel was committing to memory all the things she was too overwhelmed to absorb.

"Right, shall we take a look at you?" Doctor Arkwright said, standing.

Emily swung her legs round so she was lying flat on the bed. Daniel stood and hovered beside her. Doctor Arkwright put on some latex gloves.

"I feel like I've been abducted by aliens," Emily said, peering up at her audience.

Daniel laughed.

"Yes, you'll be prodded and poked more in the next few months than ever before in your life," Doctor Arkwright said. "By the end you'll have no qualms about stripping off in front of people. Body hang-ups go completely out the window."

"I look forward to that time," Emily said, feeling her cheeks warming with a blush.

Doctor Arkwright checked Emily's pelvis and abdomen, her hip rotations, and general joint flexibility. She moved her fingers deftly, checking almost every inch of Emily's body. Emily felt she was a lump of dough being kneaded.

"I'll order some blood tests," the doctor explained as she worked. "So we know your type and Rh status. We'll also check for anemia, certain antibodies, and make sure you're immune to all the big viruses like chickenpox, rubella, hepatitis."

Blood tests weren't exactly Emily's favorite things in the world. The thought of having so many tests made her feel increasingly anxious.

"This is your first pregnancy, isn't it, Mrs. Morey?" the doctor asked as she placed a cold stethoscope against Emily's chest.

Emily nodded. "Yes."

"Any prior gynecological problems? Abnormal pap results? Sexually transmitted infections? Anything like that?"

Emily shook her head and wondered whether it would have been better for Daniel not to have come along to this particular appointment. She'd naively thought such delicate questions wouldn't be asked immediately. She was going to have to get used to revealing everything about her body now. Nothing would be off limits!

Doctor Arkwright removed her stethoscope and slung it back around her neck again.

"Now, because of your advanced maternal age," she explained, her attention drawn back to Emily's abdomen, "it's a little more important for you to take the right vitamins, sleep enough, reduce your stress levels to the absolute minimum. They're all things we would recommend to expectant mothers whatever their age, but for you it's that extra bit important."

"Should we be worried?" Daniel asked. "About Emily's age?"

Emily frowned up at him. With her stomach on display and the both of them looking down at her like a specimen it made her feel vulnerable and somewhat at their mercy. She could cope with the doctor referring to her age, but not Daniel!

Doctor Arkwright looked at Daniel briefly and shook her head. "It's far more common for women to leave starting a family until their late thirties these days and the medical world is catching up. It's not as much an issue as it used to be. Really the main hurdle is fertility, which clearly isn't a problem in this case. There is a marginally higher risk of gestational diabetes, blood pressure problems, premature birth. But you're in safe hands."

Emily certainly felt like she was in safe hands. She just wished there wasn't so much testing to be done. It all felt a bit impersonal. Clinical. She didn't like just feeling like a baby-making vessel and would be very glad when this initial assessment was over and done with.

Doctor Arkwright peeled off her gloves. "All done. You're in good shape, so nothing of concern there. Please, take a seat and we'll have a quick look at your medical history."

Emily sat up and gave Daniel a weak smile, not quite ready to forgive him for his comments on her advanced age. She rearranged her clothes and slid her shoes back on, then took a seat. Doctor Arkwright washed her hands and then came and sat in her chair, spinning toward her computer. She took a moment to read the screen.

"You have a good clean bill of health," she said, looking through the data. "Scarlet fever in childhood with no lingering aftereffects. Non-smoker, which pleases me greatly. No particular health conditions. Nothing chronic. No ongoing medication use. A slightly higher alcohol rate than I'd like to see, but you'll be completely quitting that for the next few months anyhoo." She spun back around and looked at Emily.

"We're both quitting," Emily said.

"I didn't think it would be fair otherwise," Daniel said. "Especially since we own a bar with a cocktail waiter who's second to none!"

Doctor Arkwright smiled. Then she laid her forearms against the table and looked across at Emily, her expression serious.

"Now, this might be a little bit of a delicate thing to discuss, but I couldn't help noticing that on your registration forms you ticked the box of family history of mental health problems. If you're comfortable to do so, I'd like you to tell me a little bit more about that history. It's entirely for your benefit, no one's judging here, it's just to make sure we're keeping an eye on the right sort of things while your hormones are changing throughout the pregnancy."

Emily clasped her hands in her lap, feeling instantly uncomfortable. Talking about her chaotic upbringing was her least favorite thing to do, especially to a stranger, even if that stranger was a doctor who'd probably heard it all before and just wanted to help.

Daniel reached over and touched Emily's hand for reassurance. Buoyed by his presence, Emily took a deep breath.

"My father went through a long, long period of depression," Emily said finally, her voice sounding thin. "For dozens of years. It was following my sister's death."

Doctor Arkwright nodded and kept her face neutral as she wrote the information onto her form. "And your mother?"

"My mother?" Emily shook her head. "I don't even know what's wrong with her to be honest with you. It could be something psychiatric. But then again she might just be a difficult person."

"She's not been assessed or diagnosed with anything?"

Emily shook her head. She was feeling very uncomfortable now. Talking about this stuff always made her feel a bit panicky. But Doctor Arkwright added the information to her forms, acting in no way as if Emily's admission was anything to worry about.

"And what about yourself?" she said, gently. "Did you ever experience any problems growing up?"

Emily shrugged. "I don't think so. I mean, I was devastated after Charlotte died. And after my dad…" She stopped speaking to collect her thoughts. After a breath, she started again. "There have been some really trying times in my life. I don't know how well I dealt with them at the time. It took me years to even deal with it all. Then when I started, it came back to me in sort of scary flashbacks."

Daniel's thumb stroked the top of her hand where it was resting. "She would zone out occasionally," he added. "Sort of space out. But it happens a lot less now."

Doctor Arkwright remained very professional as they spoke, absorbing Emily's admissions with nothing more than a sympathetic nod of the head. "It sounds like you may have been experiencing some mild PTSD symptoms," she said.

Emily felt alarmed. It sounded so dramatic. For her, it had just been something she'd gone through, some kind of natural outcome to touching on the memories she'd closed off for so many years.

"Please, don't worry," the doctor reassured her. "It's far more common than people believe, particularly when trauma happens in childhood. When we don't have the language to express our emotions or even label them properly, repression becomes a natural defense mechanism. The important thing to note now is that you may be at a slightly higher risk of pre- or postnatal depression or psychosis. Again, it sounds dramatic but it's very well treated these days, through counseling and medication if necessary. As long as we keep an eye on your symptoms there's absolutely nothing to worry about."

Emily nodded and let out her breath. Doctor Arkwright was very reassuring, but at the same time she felt a sense of unpleasant anticipation for what might be in store for her. These things were never talked of. Not amongst her friends, nor her mother's generation. She couldn't help but feel worried about having a higher chance of experiencing something that was so poorly understood.

Doctor Arkwright smiled and handed a glossy folded slip of paper to Emily. "Here's a pamphlet that details nutrition, vitamins, exercise, travel do's and don'ts, et cetera. Take some time to read it and let me know if you have any questions when we next meet. I'll also give you a prescription for prenatal vitamins, which are very important. We'll book a sonogram for four weeks' time, so you can see your baby."

She turned to the computer and logged in an appointment for a scan. Then she turned back. "That's it for now. I promise the follow-ups won't take quite so long."

She stood and offered her hand to Emily to shake. Emily stood and shook the doctor's hand, and Daniel did the same. It felt like the appointment had gone so quickly and was over in a blur, though they'd been there for such a long time. Emily had no idea how much of what she'd just heard she'd managed to absorb. It felt like basically nothing.

They left the doctor's office and walked together out into the bright day.

"Did you take any of that in?" Emily asked Daniel as they strolled to where the car was parked.

"Not really," he confessed. "There was just so much information."

As they walked, Emily studied his face. He looked stressed and she wondered which bit of the appointment specifically had worried him the most. Her age-related health concerns? Her possibly elevated risk of postnatal depression? Or just the fact that he hadn't committed every single one of the doctor's words to memory?

"It's all in the pamphlet," she reassured him. "We can read it over and over again. Every night before bed, if you want."

She laughed, trying to lighten the mood. Though Daniel nodded, he still looked tense, his gaze somewhat far away. Emily wanted to ask him what was going through his mind, to find out what the issue was for certain, but he seemed to have shut down.

She felt her own excitement begin to fade away as a result. Daniel's attitude seemed to be becoming more at odds with her own. She couldn't see even the smallest flicker of excitement in his eyes. It was just concern, worry, and stress that she saw in his expression.

They got into the truck and drove home in silence.

CHAPTER THREE

Doctor Arkwright's advice for Emily to stay off her feet and reduce her stress levels to the bare minimum went immediately out the window, because Memorial Day weekend arrived all too soon and the inn was packed to the rafters.

Emily hurried down the stairs into the foyer, where guests were milling about in groups. The inn was looking beautiful thanks to Chantelle's decorations. She'd filled the place with flags. Posters for the town parade adorned every wall. It looked set to be the best event yet. Mayor Hansen had really gone above and beyond this year, with an antique fire truck procession, the marching band from the high school, and a twenty-one-gun salute at the end. Emily was glad he'd organized such a great commemoration for the men and women who'd given their lives for the country's freedom.

Lois and Marnie were on the front desk, both looking rushed off their feet as they took calls and answered guest queries. Ever since Bryony's redesign of the website had led to the inn being booked for the entire summer, Emily had had to shuffle things around. Serena wanted less work so she could focus more on her degree, so Emily had promoted Marnie from maid to front of house. Then she'd hired the Magic Elves cleaning company that Amy had sourced for the wedding to fill the void left by Marnie, and had gone on to employ an extra pair of hands in the form of a porter, a young man named Trent, whose role was to carry bags upstairs for the guests on check in. Despite the hecticness, it looked like the new system was working well. For now, at least.

Emily caught up with Bryony in the guest lounge. Her laptop was resting on her knees, a pile of half drunk cups of coffee stacked on the coffee table before her. Usually there were only ever one or two people in the guest lounge, but today every single table and couch was occupied with people drinking coffee and juice, reading papers, studying maps, and planning their days out.

"I know I say this every time I see you," Emily said to Bryony as she sat beside her, "but seriously, thank you so much for everything you've done for the inn. I've never seen it like this."

Bryony smiled. "No problem. I just can't wait until you get all the renovation work done for the expansion. It'll give me a whole load of new coding to do. New forms. New pages." Her eyes glittered with excitement.

"You really love this stuff, don't you?" Emily said, feeling baffled herself. She'd worked in marketing for years back in New York City and hated it now with every fiber of her being.

Bryony wiggled her eyebrows. "I *love* it. Plus, I get to see all the mysterious guests who book in. Look at this one." She swiveled her laptop around to show Emily the accommodation spreadsheet which was automatically populated by website bookings through the magic wizardry of computer code. "The carriage house has been booked out by Mr. X. I'm hoping he's another Roman Westbrook."

Emily raised her eyebrows, excited also. "Or a James Bond villain."

Just then, a group of three men walked into the inn. They were all wearing beige slacks and polo shirts, and had varying shades of gray hair. Emily noticed then that each had a large roll of paper under their arms and realized that they weren't some kind of traveling barbershop quartet but the architects from Erik & Sons, with their initial sketches for renovating Trevor's house.

She and Daniel had approached a local family firm, hoping they'd have a more sympathetic approach. As she leaped up now and walked toward them, she realized by their eerily similar appearances that they were the "& Sons" contingent. She shook each of their hands, blinking, feeling like she was looking at the same person three times over.

"We're triplets," the man with the lightest gray hair explained. "I'm Wayne. This is Cain. And that's Shane, the youngest by five minutes."

"My chances of remembering whose name belongs to who are more or less zero," Emily confessed.

"We don't mind," Wayne Erik continued. "We've had fifty-five years of being confused with each other. If we had a problem with it, we probably wouldn't dress the same."

He grinned, indicating their matching *Erik & Sons* navy blue polo shirts.

"Please," Emily said, "let us go and find somewhere quiet where we can spread these out. I know we're meeting for a tour of the house later today, but I'm so happy to take a look at these now."

She led them from the bustling foyer and into the empty dining room, whereby the Erik triplets unrolled their sketches onto the large walnut table.

Emily peered down at the designs, one scroll per floor of the house. The plans looked phenomenal, grand and rather exciting. But seeing Trevor's house pared down to lines and measurements on pieces of paper felt so odd to her, so unpleasant and final. She felt herself getting choked up.

"I'm sorry," she stammered, as tears suddenly sprung into her eyes. "The house belonged to my late friend. I still haven't gotten my head around the fact he's gone."

"It was Trevor Mann's house, wasn't it?" Wayne asked, softly.

"Yes," Emily said, dabbing her tears with her shirt sleeve. "Did you know him?"

"Of course," Cain confirmed. "Mr. Mann was on the zoning board so we had a lot of contact with him. He was quite a guy."

Emily could tell from the way he said it that he was being polite about the fact that Trevor was a difficult person to get along with.

"He was a curmudgeonly old so-and-so, I know," Emily said with a wistful smile. "He hated me at first. But we were great friends by the end."

The Erik brothers look at her kindly.

"We'll leave the plans with you," Wayne explained. "Then we'll talk more when we go through the house later."

"Thank you," Emily said, glad that she and Daniel had chosen to go with this firm. That they were local and knew Trevor Mann was immensely reassuring. But something about Wayne Erik's kindness made her tears come more readily. She flushed with embarrassment as she found herself suddenly unable to stop them streaming down her cheeks.

"I'm also pregnant," she confessed with a shy giggle. "The hormones are making me crazy."

The Erik triplets reassured her that she had nothing to apologize for. They left the plans with her so she and Daniel could look over them at a less hormonal moment and Emily told them she'd see them later that day.

Just then Chantelle ran into the room. Yvonne must have just dropped her home following her sleep-over with Bailey.

"Mommy!" she cried, running toward Emily and throwing her arms around her neck. She bestowed kisses onto her cheeks. "Wait, why are you crying?" she asked, moving away.

Emily wiped the tears away. "Pregnancy hormones," she said in a hushed voice. Then she put a finger to her lips.

"Our secret," Chantelle said with a nod. She jumped up off Emily's lap. "When does the Memorial Day Parade start?"

Emily checked the time. "Not long now. Once Daddy's back from the store we can all go together."

Chantelle clapped her hands. She loved a parade, and anything where she got to spend time with her friends.

Emily, too, was excited. Not just because she loved the memorial parade, but because Amy was in Sunset Harbor at the moment visiting her new boyfriend, Harry, the younger brother of Daniel's friend George. So far, Amy had kept him completely to herself. Emily was growing increasingly curious about meeting him. In fact, she'd only seen him once, before Amy had revealed they were dating, and just fleetingly. She couldn't even remember what he looked like, other than boyish. Amy was clearly in the beginning throes of lust because she'd been keeping her relationship very private, just as she had done with Fraser. Amy had a habit of not wanting any external sources to influence her relationship decisions. It had taken ages for Emily to get Amy to relent to introducing Harry, reminding Amy that she hadn't let her vet Fraser and that had ended disastrously. Amy had finally agreed that the parade was a suitable place for them to have an actual conversation, and now the time had finally arrived for Emily to meet the man who had managed to change Amy's mind about her little old town so thoroughly. She couldn't wait!

Maybe Harry was Amy's The One?

*

As expected, the town was packed with all the locals and many tourists out in force to show their respect to the troops of yore. In fact, Emily was certain she'd never seen Sunset Harbor this busy. It felt as if the place had changed quite a bit in the time she'd lived here. It wasn't as sleepy anymore.

"Is it me, or are there more people here than usual?" Daniel asked her, as they strolled along together hand in hand.

"I was just thinking the same thing," Emily said, looking about her to see if she could spot Amy and Harry anywhere in the crowd.

Just then, they saw Karen from the convenience store up ahead. They walked toward her and she turned as they drew up to her side. She hugged them all, thrilled to see them as always.

"It's so busy, isn't it?" she exclaimed, echoing their sentiments.

"More so than usual," Emily agreed.

"It's because of Roman Westbrook," Karen said, and she pointed to the other side of the road where the famous singer was waiting to watch the parade. Her eyes sparkled with excitement at the presence of the pop star on their humble streets.

Roman was standing with an entourage, something that he hadn't needed before. Emily realized that someone must have blabbed to the papers about him moving here, and she couldn't help but feel disappointed to know that word had gotten to the press so quickly. He'd been trying to keep his move here a secret to keep his privacy for as long as possible.

Emily, Chantelle, and Daniel all waved at him warmly when he looked over and saw them. Karen's eyes widened.

"You're friends?" she asked.

Emily nodded. "Even famous people chat with their neighbors, you know." Then she added, "I do hope these people aren't just here to catch a glimpse of Roman. It feels a bit… I don't know… disrespectful... to come to a memorial parade just to catch a glimpse of your favorite singer."

"It's nothing to do with Roman," Cynthia said, turning around from where she stood in front of them. Somehow, despite her neon orange hair, Emily had failed to notice her standing there with her son, Jeremy.

"What's it to do with then?" Emily asked.

"The inn!" Cynthia exclaimed. "Obviously."

Emily shook her head. "I don't think so."

But Cynthia was hearing none of it. "Believe me. After Colin Magnus wrote his article on the inn people have been buzzing about it on all the travel forums. Someone suggested Memorial weekend was a good time to visit because the parade is always so amazing. And, ba-da-boom, this is what you get."

Emily frowned, still unsure that the increase in patrons could be because of her humble inn. It was true that she'd had more bookings thanks to Colin's article. Coupled with Bryony, the marketer extraordinaire, perhaps it *was* conceivable that her inn could make this kind of impact on the town.

Emily let the news sink in and found herself grinning. She was shocked that her little inn could be helping to put Sunset Harbor on the map, but it was a good feeling. She felt proud of her achievements.

Just then, Emily noticed a familiar face in the crowd. It was Amy, looking suave in a casual black ensemble. She was holding hands with the boyishly good-looking Harry. From a distance they looked like a bit of an odd pair. Amy looked like she'd been lifted straight off the pages of *Vogue* magazine, whereas Harry was dressed more modestly. But he had a film star look about him and Emily could imagine the two of them looking very handsome together in formal attire. Emily was in no doubt that Amy would manage to change his whole sense of fashion within a matter of weeks.

"It's them," she said to Daniel, tugging on his sleeve with excitement.

She felt her stomach flip with anticipation. She wasn't entirely sure why but something felt different this time; the ease with which Amy stood beside him, the display of affection from their simple handholding which was something Amy usually resisted. There was a happiness exuding from Amy that Emily had not noticed ever before. Her excitement at getting to know Harry grew even more.

Just then, Chantelle noticed who Emily had pointed out.

"Amy!" she cried.

Ever since the bachelorette party, Chantelle had decided she liked Amy, and had gotten over their initial rocky introduction when she'd thought Amy and Jayne were New York snobs.

As Chantelle careened toward Amy, Amy turned and bent down just in time to catch Chantelle in her arms. Looking a little surprised, she straightened up and twirled the little girl in a circle, somehow managing to keep her balance in her chic black heels.

Daniel and Emily wended their way through the crowds as Amy popped Chantelle back down on her feet. They stopped beside her and Amy became instantly red.

Emily hugged her friend tightly. Then, as she released her from the embrace, she caught her eye and wiggled her eyebrows.

Amy's blush deepened. "Em, Daniel, this is Harry. Harry, my best friend Emily and her husband, Daniel."

Daniel shook Harry's hand. "We've met before," he explained. "I'm an old friend of George's."

"Of course!" Harry said, his eyes widening with surprise. "But it was a long time ago now."

Daniel nodded. "I spent some years in Tennessee."

Chantelle looked up at Harry and beamed then. "That's where I get my accent from," she said.

Harry smiled at her, seemingly taken by her spirit. Emily noticed his fingers re-entwining with Amy's. She felt a smile tugging at the corner of her lips.

Behind them, the flag parade streamed past. Then the thirty-strong marching band started, blaring out "Hail to the Spirit of Liberty" in trumpets, French horns, and woodwinds. The crowd surged toward the road to get a better look.

"Do you come to the parade often?" Emily asked Harry as people filtered past her. She was eager to know more about him.

"Of course, every year," Harry explained. "We come from military ancestry. Both on our mom's side and on our dad's side. So it means a lot to both George and I."

Emily wanted to speak to him further but the band was fast approaching and the noise was too great. She fell silent and watched them, thinking, as she was here to do, of all the fallen men and women.

At last the band passed, but the noise didn't lessen because hot on their heels came the antique fire truck procession, their bells clanging. It was a long stream of them, not just fire trucks but old military tanks, too, clanking and rattling along the road on caterpillar treads. It was quite a sight to behold. And with the heaving crowds, it felt very loud and chaotic. Emily wondered if her overwhelmed feeling was partly from the pregnancy hormones heightening her senses.

"We have to follow them to the park now," Chantelle said, grabbing Emily's hand. " That's where they're doing the gun salute. Quick! I don't want to miss it!"

She tugged, and Emily followed her. The huge crowd of people who'd been watching streamed into the park. Emily felt like she was in a river of people flowing along the streets, caught in a current. It was a somewhat claustrophobic feeling. The only thing grounding her was Chantelle's hand squeezing hers tightly.

She looked around, searching for Daniel, Amy, and Harry. She caught sight of them being herded along with the flow of people.

Harry was looking adoringly at Amy, a protective arm around her shoulders. Her expression was serene, as though she were completely lost in her happiness. Emily smiled again, realizing that Amy was completely smitten. She couldn't wait to learn more about Harry once the noise and furor had died down.

As the crowds reached the park and dispersed, the others caught up with them. They huddled around the group of military personnel in uniforms, who had their guns pointed to the sky. Emily felt a sudden sense of anxiety at the thought of the loud noise. Though she knew it was perfectly safe she couldn't help but worry now, knowing that it was more than her own safety that mattered. The power of her maternal instinct to protect her unborn child almost took her by surprise.

"Let's stand a little way back," she said aloud, hovering a foot or so behind the crowds, trying to take a step backward.

"But I can't see," Chantelle complained. She bobbed up and down on her tiptoes, frowning, eager to get nearer to the action.

"Daniel, can you take her closer?" Emily asked, finally staggering back enough to be beside the benches. She gripped the back of one to steady herself as a panicky sensation swept through her.

"But I want us to go to the front together," Chantelle said, her voice verging on whining.

Daniel knelt down and looked Chantelle in the eye. Emily overheard him say in a hushed voice, "Remember our secret? Emily needs to be here, at the back. So either you come to the front with just me, or we all stay together. You can climb on the bench or get on my shoulders if you want a better view."

Chantelle wasn't to be convinced. She folded her arms petulantly and pouted.

"I didn't know the baby meant we wouldn't be able to have fun anymore," she grumbled.

Emily tensed. Not because she was worried about Harry and Amy overhearing—she was certain with the volume of chatter they wouldn't be able to pick Chantelle's voice out of the crowd—but because she felt bad to have dampened Chantelle's spirits. She didn't want there to be any competition or animosity between Chantelle and the new baby. It mattered to her greatly that they had a harmonious family life. She hoped this was just a moment of teething problems, something that wouldn't grow.

“Chantelle,” Daniel warned, clearly not impressed with her attitude.

Suddenly, the guns started firing. The noise was immense. Emily covered her ears with her hands, alarmed and exhilarated by the sheer volume. The crowd was stunned into silence as the explosive sound cracked through the sky. It felt as if everyone was gasping collectively.

Then the firing stopped and everyone began to clap and cheer.

Amy turned to face them, her eyes bright with exhilaration. “Wow, that was awesome,” she beamed.

Emily nodded, glad to see Amy had enjoyed her small-town parade experience. But she still hadn’t had a chance to speak to Harry and she was desperate to know more about him.

“We should all go and get lunch,” Emily suggested.

Even though Emily was feeling a little nauseous and the idea of lunch made her stomach turn, she didn’t want Amy to hurry off with Harry and deny her the chance to speak to him properly.

Chantelle cheered up instantly at the suggestion. Everyone agreed it was a good idea.

As they left the crowds behind and ambled slowly along the roads, Emily wondered how well she’d be able to refrain from blurting out the news of her pregnancy to her closest friend. But then she realized that Amy would likely guess all on her own. Not just because she was intuitive but because all it would probably take was for Emily to turn down a glass of wine for her to guess. She felt a sudden sense of excitement as she realized that very soon someone she dearly loved would be party to her news.

She couldn’t wait to see Amy’s reaction.

CHAPTER FOUR

As part of the Memorial parade, an outside barbecue had been set up, with picnic benches to eat at. Emily thought it a rather fitting test for Amy, who was so used to dining in swanky New York City establishments. But Harry was a local, like Daniel, like she and Chantelle had now become, and he was enthusiastic about the prospect of eating outside. Emily noted the way Amy looked visibly distressed as it dawned on her that she was the odd one out and wouldn't be able to persuade anyone to eat elsewhere.

They took one of the benches at the end of the row, furthest from the busy streets, the music, and celebrations, where it was quieter. Daniel and Harry went off to order them all hot dogs and soda, leaving Chantelle, Amy, and Emily to catch up.

"It's so nice to see you," Emily said to Amy. "And to see you so happy," she added, knowingly.

Amy blushed and replied rather stiltedly, "Yes. Well."

"You fit in with the Sunset Harbor crowd now," Chantelle said with a grin.

Emily smirked. "I agree wholeheartedly. You're right at home here."

Amy's blush deepened. She was clearly very uncomfortable with the whole situation.

Soon, Daniel and Harry returned with the food, both chatting happily like they were old friends. They sat down and handed everyone a paper plate with a hot dog.

"So Harry," Emily began, excited to finally be able to query him and get to know him. "What job do you do? Are you in glass restoration like George?"

Out the corner of her eye she noticed Amy's expression turn to horror. Emily smirked to herself. It was exactly the sort of question Amy had fired at all of her past boyfriends so it seemed only fair that Emily gave her a taste of her own medicine. And anyway, she was genuinely curious. Amy had pretty high standards when it came to the earning potential of her partners. If Harry bucked the trend of being a high-flier, as Emily suspected, it would be even more evidence that Amy was finally properly in love rather than treating her relationships like a business partnership.

"Construction, actually," Harry explained. "My firm specializes in sprucing up properties. We mainly modernize old houses before selling them."

"I could've done with knowing you a couple years back," Emily joked, remembering the hard work of getting the inn into shape. "Do you enjoy the work?" she added, although really she wanted to be nosy and find out how much he earned.

"I do, but I've been doing it for a while now and I'm getting itchy feet," Harry said. "I'm hoping to change jobs. I want to be my own employer, open a business."

Emily was impressed with his ambition. She couldn't imagine Amy being happy with a construction worker, but she could certainly see her settling down with an entrepreneur.

"What kind of business?" Daniel asked, curious.

"Well, the dream is to open a restaurant," Harry said. "I've been waiting for the right moment, though. In a place like Sunset Harbor a lot of the business can be seasonal. But things are just starting to change. There are more tourists, and I think we could handle another one."

Emily's eyes glittered as she glanced over at Daniel. "Competition," she joked.

Harry was midway through a mouthful of hot dog. His eyebrows rose as he chewed more hurriedly. He swallowed. "You're opening a restaurant, too?" he asked, surprised.

Emily dipped the end of her hot dog in a mound of ketchup. "We already serve food at the inn for guests, and the speakeasy is open to the public. But we're planning to further expand over the summer and have a larger restaurant that serves high-end evening meals, open to the public rather than just guests. Our friends the Bradshaws own the fish restaurant in town so they're going to give us some advice. I could put you in touch with them if you'd like."

Harry looked thrilled. "That would be amazing. Thanks." Then he looked over at Amy. "I didn't realize your friends would be my business rivals."

Emily laughed. "Nonsense. I was only joking. We all help each other out here! And now is definitely a good time to open more eateries."

"You think the town can handle more?" Harry asked, looking genuinely interested in Emily's take on the subject.

She felt proud to be in a position to be offering advice to others now, when not that long ago she'd been the one needing expertise. "I do," she said. "And we don't have to compete. We could work together to make the good folk of Sunset Harbor want to eat out more than once a month! The people around here can be quite humble and dining out a lot seems flashy to them. Together we could turn that around."

Harry looked more and more interested. Emily felt herself warming to him. He seemed to have real spirit, a sparkle in his eye, a hunger to experience more and reach for the stars. She could see what Amy saw in him—other than his film star good looks and the builder's physique she presumed he had hidden beneath his shirt. Amy was beaming with pride next to him.

"Here's an idea," Daniel said, suddenly alight with enthusiasm. "Maybe you could run our restaurant instead of us employing a manager. Get some experience under your belt for when you decide to go it alone."

"Daniel," Emily hissed out the corner of her mouth. "That's a bit forward."

But Harry looked delighted. "That would be amazing," he said. "I've been stuck in construction for ages not knowing how to break out, or when to time it, or how to even approach it. If there's a job for me to move into it wouldn't be so terrifying!"

"Let's definitely keep that option open then," Emily agreed.

She didn't want to rush into anything. They had only just met, after all. And though she felt an immediate friendly connection with Harry she had to keep it at the back of her mind that things might not remain all sunshine and roses between him and Amy forever. What if they had a messy breakup? It would be awful for Amy every time she visited knowing her ex was onsite. Best not to rush into anything, though Emily had a strange feeling in her bones that told her it was a great idea, that Harry had landed in their life at this exact moment for this exact reason.

"Are you looking for investors for your expansion?" Amy asked. "I'm looking to broaden my portfolio and you guys seem like a great bet."

Emily was shocked by the offer. Though Amy was always offering positions at her business to her friends, she was cautious when it came to mixing friendship and money. She'd been burned in the past when lending to friends and didn't do it often anymore.

Suddenly, Chantelle let out a frustrated groan. "This is *boring*!" she wailed. "Can we please stop talking about business?"

Everyone laughed. Emily nodded to Amy. "Let's discuss it another time."

Amy smiled. "Sure."

Emily looked again at Harry. "So did you go to college here in Maine?"

"No, actually I went abroad instead," Harry said. "I was supposed to spend a month building homes in Ghana but I ended up staying for eight months."

Emily's eyes widened with surprise. "How fascinating!"

Harry smiled. "It was great. I loved the hands-on work. It was hard going, digging trenches, laying foundations, building tanks for water, but it was so satisfying. And I met so many great people. My parents thought it was a bit of a strange thing to do voluntarily, though. I think they would have preferred that if I wasn't going to college I at least earned some money."

"Do you get on well with your parents? With George?"

Harry nodded. "Oh yeah, we're very close. They can just be a bit traditional sometimes. They wanted us both to go to college, get sensible jobs, marry, have kids. So far neither of us have followed the path they were intending."

Chantelle piped up then. "Well, when you marry Amy they'll get their wish."

Emily laughed loudly. Amy's eyes darted to the table. But Harry took Chantelle's comment in good spirits. Emily found herself liking him more and more. She had no time for men who acted terrified by the very thought of commitment. Harry had definitely passed that initial test with flying colors.

Amy turned to Chantelle, clearly wanting to steer the course of the conversation away from her budding relationship. "Right, it's your turn. What's happening in the world of Chantelle? Any exciting news? Any secrets?"

Chantelle's eyes widened at the mention of the word "secret" and Emily could tell her mind had instantly gone to the pregnancy, which they taken great pains to explain to her was a secret.

Feeling jovial from the meal, Emily decided that telling Amy wouldn't be such a bad idea. She wiggled her eyebrows at Chantelle.

"I think you can let Amy know about your secret," she said, grinning.

Daniel touched Emily's hand over the table. "You sure?" he queried.

Emily nodded. Amy looked from one to the other, her eyes squinting suspiciously.

"Tell me right now," she demanded. "The anticipation is killing me!"

Chantelle looked like a balloon about to pop with excitement. She gave Daniel and Emily each one last glance for confirmation that she was really allowed to spill the news. When they both nodded, she looked back at Amy, bounced up and down in her seat and squeezed her hands together.

"Mommy's pregnant!" she cried.

Then she instantly clapped her hands over her mouth and looked around to make sure no one else had overheard her exclamation.

Amy's face transformed into an expression of euphoria. "You are? Oh my God! Em!" Then she burst out crying.

Emily was surprised. Amy wasn't one to cry readily. The sight of her so emotional like that made Emily well up as well.

"Don't! You're setting off my hormones again," she exclaimed.

Amy leapt up from her seat and ran around to Emily, grabbing her in an embrace.

"I'm so happy for you!" she cried.

The two friends hugged tightly. In her peripheral vision, Emily noticed Harry congratulating Daniel with a handshake.

Amy let go and finally composed herself, wiping her tears away. Then she hugged Daniel too.

"Congratulations," she said. Finally, she sat back down and squeezed Chantelle around the shoulders. "You're going to be a big sister, huh?"

Chantelle nodded vigorously. "Not until December though, which is forever to wait."

Amy quickly counted back on her fingers. "December? When did you conceive?"

Emily flushed red. "Not a topic for the dinner table, Ames," she said.

Amy's eyes widened and she mouthed, "Honeymoon?"

Emily nodded and turned her gaze down.

"What are you saying?" Chantelle asked, looking between the two women. She looked at Daniel. "Daddy, what are they whispering about?"

Daniel laughed. "Nothing, sweetie. We'll tell you another time. When you're a little older."

Chantelle folded her arms and pouted. Everyone laughed.

"Oh, Em," Amy gushed. "My cheeks hurt from smiling so much. Will you let me take you shopping to get a gift for the baby?"

"Now?" Emily asked.

"Yes!" Amy exclaimed. "I'm too excited to wait. I'll drive us up to Bangor. There is a gorgeous bespoke baby store there. What do you say?"

Emily looked at Daniel and Chantelle. "Do you guys mind?"

"Not at all," Daniel said. "I'll take Chantelle home for singing practice."

He stood then and everyone followed suit.

"Harry, it was great to meet you," Daniel said, shaking Harry's hand again. "Let's stay in touch about the restaurant stuff, okay? Maybe hang out with George sometime. I've sworn off alcohol for the duration of Emily's pregnancy but we could do something else. Do you fish?"

"I love to fish," Harry said, grinning.

"Great, we'll go out on my boat sometime," Daniel told him.

They exchanged numbers, and Emily felt like the two of them in particular had hit it off. It made her so happy to see. Fraser and Daniel were never going to be friends, they were from such different worlds. But with Harry she could easily see the four of them hanging out on the porch, drinking together, enjoying local events with each other. She could suddenly picture the future, with Harry and Amy married, settled in the neighborhood, their kids at the same school as Emily and Daniel's. It was an awesome thought!

Emily said farewell to Harry and Chantelle, then Amy looped her arm around Emily's and dragged her off to the car, bouncing with every step, exclaiming in every way possible just how happy she was for her friend.

"Can I be godmother?" she asked.

"Maybe, but that wouldn't be fair to Jayne."

"Jayne wouldn't want to be a godmother."

"No, but she'd still kick up a fuss and you know it."

"Fine. In which case, if it's a girl can it be named Amy?"

Emily laughed and shrugged. "We haven't discussed names yet. You do know Daniel gets an equal say. And, *again,* I must stress that Jayne would be livid if I called the baby Amy!"

Amy moved on quickly to her next excited exclamation. “When he or she grows up they can come and intern with me! I’ll be cool Aunt Amy with the apartment in New York.”

Emily just nodded along to all of her exclamations, overjoyed that Amy was so openly happy for her. They had come so far since that time when Amy had been furious with her for running away from New York City. Now it felt like they were closer than ever, like their bond was unbreakable. Emily just hoped that things went so well with Harry that Amy moved closer. Then, everything truly would be perfect.

CHAPTER FIVE

Typically of Amy, Emily found herself being dragged into the most high-end, luxurious children's store imaginable. It was all beech wood shelving and pastel-colored walls, hundred-dollar quilts and thousand-dollar christening gifts. It stocked everything from clothes and gadgets to baby furniture and ornaments.

"Amy, you can't get me a gift from here," Emily protested, glancing about her at all the beautiful items.

"Why not?" Amy retorted. "My best friend is having a baby. I can spoil you as much as I want. Now do you want something practical like a stroller or something lavish like this organic eco-friendly pacifier? Ooh look!" Amy cried, becoming instantly distracted and hurrying over to another shelf. "Biodegradable diapers." She grabbed a packet and began reading off the back. "Hypo-allergenic materials. Rainforest alliance certified. Low toxins. No dyes."

Emily felt a little overwhelmed by the choices available to her. She hadn't even begun to think about toxins or allergens. She'd hardly even thought about diapers and pacifiers! She'd only just begun to wrap her head around the fact a baby the size of a raspberry was currently growing inside of her.

"How much stuff is this baby going to need?" Emily said, suddenly feeling anxious.

Amy looked at her friend, concerned. "Don't start freaking out."

"But I haven't even begun to work it all out," Emily replied, hearing her own voice rising with panic.

Amy sprung into action. She scooped an arm around Emily's shoulder and led her to a plush Scandinavian-style nursing armchair—that cost $1,400 dollars, Emily read on the sign—and sat her down.

"Let's make a list," Amy said. She perched on the matching charcoal footstool opposite Emily and looked up. "There's nothing like a list for clearing the mind."

Emily shook her head. "I don't need a list," she said with a resigned giggle. "I'm just having a moment. It's all so new and strange and… unexpected."

"It wasn't planned then?" Amy asked, curiously. "The baby, I mean?"

"Nope," Emily confessed. "But if I *did* conceive on our honeymoon like we all seem to think, then it must have been the night before Daniel told me he wanted to start trying for a baby." She chewed her lip, remembering how Daniel had booked the entire lighthouse restaurant in order to broach the subject in a beautiful and romantic way, and how terribly that moment had ended for them when she suddenly got cold feet. "Right before I told him I wasn't ready."

"Oh…" Amy said, wrinkling her nose. Her voice softened. "You didn't want this to happen?"

"I did," Emily said. "I changed my mind a couple of weeks later. I just needed some time to let it sink in. But I must have already been pregnant by then so I wonder if it was just the hormones changing my mind subliminally. And I think the damage was done by that point, for Daniel, I mean. He seemed glad when I told him I'd changed my mind again but I wonder whether he kept hold of a bit of resentment."

"The pregnancy isn't quite as happy a surprise for him as it is for you?" Amy asked.

Emily shrugged. She became aware of all the fears she'd been bottling up. "I was the more reticent but now that it's here it feels so perfect and right. But Daniel just seems stressed. Like there's something he's not telling me. I was wondering if it was something to do with how much he missed out on Chantelle's start in life. But he's being typical Daniel about it. Not saying a word. Leaving me to speculate."

Amy patted Emily's hand. "I'm sorry, Em. That sounds hard. And you could do without that kind of stress right now."

Emily smiled at her friend. "I actually feel a ton better now I've talked to you about it. It's so nice having you here." She wiggled her eyebrows. "So, Harry. Do you think this is the real deal?"

Amy blushed as the conversation turned, once again, toward her blossoming romance with Harry.

"It's going really well," she confessed. "We're so different yet somehow so completely compatible."

Emily grinned. "I always had a feeling you needed a younger man."

"Oh, don't remind me," Amy said, rolling her eyes. "He's only five years younger than me but it feels like a whole generation. I'll mention some pop song that I liked in high school and he'll tell me he remembers it from when he was ten! I mean he's still closer to his twenties than his forties."

"I don't think thirty-six should be counted as being close to your forties," Emily said, remembering her own classification as an older mother and the slight risk it posed her. She always felt a little sensitive when people brought up aging, even if accidentally.

"Fine," Amy said. "But thirty-one sounds like a baby to me! I don't like to think about it. Me hitting the big four-oh so much sooner than him."

"You're thinking that far ahead?" Emily asked, raising her eyebrows.

Amy shrugged. "I guess I am. I can't help it. We just click. It's like everything is easy, you know. Even the arguments don't feel that bad because I just have this sense that we'll work it out."

"That's amazing," Emily said, smiling to herself. Amy's description sounded just like her own relationship with Daniel. It wasn't easy, there were still challenges, but there was a pervading sense that they would make it work no matter what. "But what do you argue about?"

"Time," Amy said. "Distance. Obviously."

"Yeah, what's going to happen with that?" Emily asked. "Do you think you'll move here? Or Harry to New York City?"

"I don't know. I'm here for the summer now so I'm just going to think about that. I needed to get out of the city for a bit anyway. I guess I'll see how I feel about it after having spent a couple of months here. The back and forth wasn't fun but I wonder if once the initial passion stage dies down a bit the long distance might not be so much of an issue anymore."

Emily laughed. "It's so funny hearing you speak like this. There was a point when a weekend was too long for you here."

Amy looked embarrassed. "Well, it was," she said defensively. "Back then. Things are different now."

"You're in love," Emily pointed out. "Now you know why I had to stay here."

Amy nodded reluctantly. She hated being wrong.

Just then, the store woman came over. "I'm sorry, ladies," she said, "but we're closing now. Did you want to purchase anything before I shut down the till?"

"No thanks," Emily said at exactly the same time as Amy said, "Yes."

Emily looked at her friend, frowning with confusion.

"We'll have this nursing seat," Amy said.

"Ames, no way!" Emily cried. "It's so expensive!"

Amy shook her head. "It's fine. You deserve it. And it already has significance to us. We had a good heart-to-heart on this very chair. We can't not take it now that it has such sentimental value."

Emily held her hands up, relenting. There was no point arguing with Amy over this. Best to just let her friend go all out. Treating her friends was one of her great pleasures in life after all.

They paid for the chair and loaded it into the back of Amy's car. Emily noticed as she got in the passenger's seat that she had a missed call from the inn. She checked her voicemail. It was Lois.

"Sorry to disturb you, Emily, but the Erik & Sons men are here. They said they had a meeting booked with you. A tour of Trevor's house. Daniel says you have the keys so he can't let them in."

"Oh no!" Emily cried. "Amy, floor it. I'm late for a meeting!"

CHAPTER SIX

The echo inside Trevor's house made Emily shudder. It felt so empty and unlived in. So devoid of humanness.

Wayne Erik drew up to Emily's side. "It's a beautiful place," he said. "Trevor kept it in great condition."

"It was his summer home for many years before he moved in full time," Emily explained. "That might account for the lack of wear and tear."

That and the fact that Trevor hadn't really had anyone in his life; no family or friends to visit him. He'd rattled around in that big house alone for years. Emily wondered whether her father lived a similar type of existence. Elderly and alone. Maybe he had neighbors who thought he'd been abandoned by his family, who worried about him getting lonely. The thought made her ache inside.

Daniel came up next to her and touched her elbow lightly. "Are you okay?" he asked softly.

Emily nodded. "I just get so sad when I come here," she explained.

Daniel scooped his arm around her shoulder. "I know. It's a good thing that we're transforming it. Although I know it doesn't always feel like we're doing the right thing by stripping Trevor from this place. But you did it with the inn, remember, and that was ultimately the best decision."

"You're right," Emily agreed.

They held hands as they walked through the house together with the architects, stopping periodically to study their plans and compare them with the real thing. The Erik brothers had drawn up several options for how to convert the house, depending on how many rooms Emily and Daniel decided on as guest bedrooms, how big they wanted the restaurant and open-plan kitchen area to be, and how much they were willing to spend. The cheapest option involved doing the least amount of work, keeping at many of the original internal walls in place as possible, but Emily was certain she wanted the entirety of the lower floor to be completely open plan, which was only a feature on the most expensive option. From a business plan point of view, they also had to factor in the increase of income from having more rooms to rent out, but Emily didn't want to just cram in as many as possible. The third floor of the inn already had dozens of smaller, cheaper rooms. Emily wanted this part of the inn to be luxurious, high end, something that would really dazzle visitors.

They stopped in the kitchen and looked over the three plans.

"I want this to be the lower floor," Emily explained, pointing at Wayne's creation for the kitchen and restaurant. "But this for the rooms." She pointed at Cain's third-floor plan with just three apartment-style rooms that could accommodate families with space for a living room and separate bathroom in each apartment. "I like how you've laid them out so that each one has an ocean view."

Daniel seemed to agree, though Emily noticed his focus was much more on the cost of things. It hadn't escaped his notice that she'd chosen the most expensive downstairs option and the least lucrative upstairs option.

"And what about the second floor?" Wayne Erik asked.

"I can't decide," Emily explained. More bedrooms as per Shane's design? Or more restaurant space as per Wayne's? "What if we were to replicate the third floor on the second?" she said. "A carbon copy?"

Daniel frowned. "But then there would only be six apartments in the whole house," he interjected.

"I know," Emily explained. "But think of it in terms of the revenue from the higher price of the apartments. Right now there's only one place for families to stay, which is the carriage house. But Bryony said there was so much demand coming in from families who want to spend the summer in Sunset Harbor. If we convert this into the family-friendly part of the inn it would be a great selling point. Plus, if we do it this way then every room can be advertised as having an ocean view! That would be an amazing selling point too."

"I can see what you're saying," Daniel said, not sounding even the slightest bit convinced. "But I can't help feeling like that's not the best use of the space."

"We'd only need to have six families each summer to get fully booked," Emily contested.

"We don't want to get fully booked from six families," Daniel countered. "If there's so much demand, why not double the amount of apartments? Income from twelve families is going to be better than just from six!"

Emily rubbed her forehead. She didn't just want to pack the inn to the brim. And more people traipsing in and out would mean hiring more staff to care for them. They would cause more damage and wear and tear that she'd need to account for. The costs would be eradicated through the amount of cleaning, reupholstering and towel washing alone!

"We can always go back to the drawing board," Wayne said. "Find a compromise that's somewhere between your two ideas."

"Like what?" Emily asked, not sure that there could be a compromise to satisfy both her desire to keep the inn feeling personal while making it as luxurious as possible with Daniel's wish for a more stable income.

"We could make six smaller apartments on the second floor," he said. "Then you can get a range of prices as well."

"But what about the ocean views?" Emily asked. She desperately wanted every room to look out over the gorgeous sea.

"We could try to design them so that as many as possible had a view. But it would be impossible for all of them to. Probably three. Four at the most."

Emily knew that it would make things a little more complicated when it came to the booking forms on the website, but Bryony would probably relish the challenge so that shouldn't be too much of an issue.

Wayne spoke again. "Why don't we create the new designs over the next few days and you can see what you think?"

Emily looked at Daniel for an opinion. He just gave a little shrug. She turned back to Wayne.

"We may as well try some new designs," she said.

"Sure," Wayne replied. "The rest of the work we can get started on right away, though."

"When do you think we'll be able to get all the work done by?" Daniel asked.

Wayne Erik looked down at the plans spread on the table and pondered. "Considering we're going to redraw this floor," he said, pointing at the second floor, "we're probably looking at Labor Day for the whole thing to be complete."

"That soon?" Emily asked, surprised. She'd been expecting years of work.

"Yes, for this place," Wayne explained. "For the spa over at the inn it may take a little longer as you'll need different constructors in there. Pool specialists and the like."

Emily had quite forgotten about Chantelle's spa plan to transform the empty old swimming pool. She realized then that they hadn't yet looked at the brothers' options for converting that place

"Can we look over those designs now?" Emily asked.

"Of course," Wayne said.

"We should fetch Chantelle," Emily said to Daniel. "It was her idea, she should be involved."

They left Trevor's house and collected Chantelle from the inn. Then they all went into the dark, unused outhouse that stood on the inn's grounds. It was cold inside, despite the warm weather, dark and filled with shadows. Emily was glad for the sensation of Chantelle's warm hand in hers, and drew comfort from it.

The brothers produced their plans for Emily, Chantelle, and Daniel to consider. The most impressive (and, once again, the most expensive) was to convert the space into a part indoor and part outdoor spa, overlooking the ocean. The barn area in that specific design would have two floors, a spiral staircase connecting the two, and the top floor containing an infinity pool with views of the oceans.

"I can't resist the staircase," Emily said. She'd wanted one ever since she'd set eyes on the yacht club's.

Daniel grew animated then. "We could design it. The team at Jack Cooper's, I mean. We've done spiral staircases before and it would help keep costs down. In fact"—he looked again at the plans and Wayne's lightly scribbled notes—"we could do this paneling work here as well. The changing area doors. The reception desk."

He looked excited by the prospect and Emily was glad to see that glint in his eye once more. He'd seemed so stressed recently it was good to just see him enthusiastic again.

"And if we hire Jack Cooper's for the woodwork then I'll be onsite, closer to home," he added. "I can project manage the whole thing."

"I like the sound of that," Emily said, thinking of the baby and how much more relaxed she felt knowing Daniel was close by as opposed to the other side of town. Not that she was anticipating going into labor anytime soon!

Chantelle nodded her agreement. "It would make it even more special to know you'd made some of it yourself," she said.

With the decision made, they bade farewell to the architects from Erik & Sons and went back to the inn. As they crossed the lawn, Emily was happy listening to Chantelle and Daniel's merry chatter and all their grand ideas. But as they went, Emily couldn't help notice the disparity between how excited Daniel seemed about the renovation work in comparison to how stressed and muted he seemed about the baby.

When they reached the inn, Emily was so wrapped up in her thoughts she'd become completely distracted. Her main focus in life at the moment was the baby; it was the main source of her excitement, the thing that she thought of last thing at night and first thing in the morning. But she felt like that wasn't the case for Daniel. He seemed more enthusiastic about making a wooden spiral staircase!

"I think I'm going to head upstairs for a rest," Emily said, wanting to excuse herself and take some time to sit with her thoughts alone.

She went up to her room and sat on her vanity stool, staring at her reflection in the mirror. Why was Daniel behaving this way? Amy had acted a hundred times more enthusiastic when she'd told her. Amy had wanted to instantly run out and buy things for the nursery, but Daniel hadn't even mentioned all the things they would need for the baby. Even if he went into his practical, logical, sensible mode and started researching strollers and car seats that would be better than the overwhelmed and slightly stressed state he seemed to be in.

As she mulled on her thoughts, Emily realized then that the only people other than immediate family who even knew about the baby were Amy and Harry. She'd told a friend but hadn't yet told the person she wanted to the most, the person whose reaction would be the best of all: her dad.

She rummaged in her drawer for some paper and pen. Knowing full well that her father had next to no connection to the internet, and only a pay phone in the village which would be difficult to coordinate, she knew that writing to him would be the quickest way to get him the news. Plus, there was something extra special about writing an old-school letter. He could keep it and cherish it for years to come. Holding onto scraps of paper was one of her father's great pleasures, after all.

She began to write.

Dear Dad,

I miss you so much! The house just isn't the same without you. Coming home after the honeymoon was bittersweet because I knew that you wouldn't be here. I hope we can fly out to England to see you this summer as you suggested. I know Chantelle would love that. She's pining for her Papa Roy!

My reason for writing to you is actually two-fold. I'm not just writing to tell you how much I miss having you around, but because I also have some exciting news. Daniel and I have recently discovered that I'm pregnant! Can you believe it? You're going to be a granddad! The due date has been set for early December.

Of course I would prefer to have been able to tell you my news in person but I thought this would be the best way to get the news to you. Plus you can frame this letter or add it to your hoards of paper, which I know you're fond of doing!

I look forward to getting your return letter. Or, even better, you could invest in a cell phone and then we could FaceTime! Video calls, Dad, can you believe it? It's like we're living in the future!

All my love, always, forever,

Emily Jane xx

She read the letter again, hoping Roy would appreciate her slightly cheeky tone and not be offended by it, then folded it up and put it in an envelope.

Just then, Emily heard a knock on the door. She turned to see Chantelle poking her head around.

"What's wrong, Mommy?" she asked. "You've been up here for ages."

Emily gestured for her to enter and the little girl walked inside, padding across the rug with soft footsteps. When she reached Emily she folded into her open arms.

"Nothing's wrong," Emily told the little girl. "I just wanted to write a letter to Papa Roy to tell him about the baby." She held up the now sealed envelope. "Would you like to come and mail this with me?"

Chantelle nodded her agreement. Emily handed her the envelope, which she clutched in her hand, then they left Emily's room together. They went downstairs and out the front door, then headed along the lane slowly toward the mailbox, hand in hand. Emily noticed that Chantelle was awfully quiet as they went.

Usually the child never stopped talking, but she hadn't uttered a word since they'd left the B&B.

"Are you okay, love?" Emily asked, giving her hand a little squeeze.

Chantelle looked up at her sadly, her other hand tightly clutching the envelope. "I miss Papa Roy," she said.

"I do too," Emily replied wistfully.

"Doesn't Papa Roy have a phone we can call him on?" Chantelle asked. "We could do a FaceTime call?"

Emily laughed and tapped the envelope. "I asked him the very same thing in that letter," she said. But despite her attempt to lighten the mood, she couldn't help but share in Chantelle's disappointment. Getting a cell phone was the last thing she could imagine her father doing.

"He did say he might get a phone," Chantelle said. "Remember?"

Emily did. Just before they'd left for Martha's Vineyard. She'd been wishing him goodbye, something she hadn't had the chance to do since the age of fifteen, and he'd joked that he might get a phone to keep in better contact. At the time she'd felt filled with hope. Not that he'd get a phone but that he would remain in regular contact. Sadly, it didn't seem to be panning out that way. If he couldn't stay in letter touch, what chance was there of him breaking with the habit of a lifetime and getting a phone!

"I'm going to pray that he does get one," Chantelle said affirmatively. "And that we get to FaceTime each other."

Emily nodded, hiding the grief that was creeping up inside of her. "I think that's a very good idea," she told the child.

Chantelle closed her eyes and Emily watched, her heart swelling, as the girl's lips moved in silent prayer. Then she opened her eyes and grinned. "Amen."

They reached the mailbox and Emily helped Chantelle put the letter inside. As they headed back to the house, Emily heard an incoming text message on her cell. She instantly thought of her father. Perhaps Chantelle's prayer had been answered already!

But when she pulled her phone out of her pocket she was surprised to see that the name on the screen was Roman Westbrook.

Emily felt a jolt of shock. She didn't want to act star-struck around Roman at all. He'd made it very clear how important his privacy was, how much he appreciated being respected in Sunset Harbor. It was among his reasons for wanting to stay in contact with

Emily and the rest of the family after checking out. But she also couldn't quite get her head around the fact that *Roman Westbrook,* famous singer, mega superstar, was a contact in her phone!

She opened the message and read it in her head, then exclaimed aloud.

"What is it?" Chantelle asked quizzically.

"Roman's bought his house," Emily said to Chantelle. "The one in Sunset Harbor."

"Cool," Chantelle said. "Does that mean we can do a welcome party? Take him a gift basket?"

Chantelle loved making up packages for the neighbors. She'd created several care packages for Trevor when he'd still been alive.

"He wants us to come over for a dinner party," Emily told the child.

Chantelle looked excited and clapped her hands. "When? When?"

"Today!" Emily exclaimed. "Quick, go and put on a nice dress and wash your face. I'll get Daddy!"

They hurried back to the inn, both as excited as each other that they would be spending the evening with none other than Roman Westbrook.

CHAPTER SEVEN

Of course Roman's house was in the nicest part of Sunset Harbor. Emily felt a little embarrassed as they pulled onto the curved driveway in Daniel's beat-up, rattling pickup truck.

"We really need a new car," she said, looking out the passenger's side window and up at the huge, vast mansion.

Chantelle whistled. "This place is awesome," she said.

There were pots containing styled topiary, creeping ivy and roses up the walls, a *fountain,* and Roman's cream-colored Rolls Royce parked to one side.

The family got out of the pickup truck and went to the large, carved front door. Chantelle rang the bell and a few seconds later it was opened by a humongous security man wearing a dark suit and a very stern expression.

"I'm Emily Morey," Emily explained. "This is my husband, Daniel, and our daughter, Chantelle."

The man didn't say a word but he nodded as though he'd been briefed on their arrival and stepped aside. They went through the door and into the foyer, which had vast ceilings and pristine tiled floors. The decor inside was far more modern than the outside would have suggested.

They were greeted next by a maid, a young East Asian woman dressed casually in a summer dress. She took their coats and slung them over her arm.

"Can I show you through to the drawing room? Mr. Westbrook won't be a moment."

They followed her into a large room with wooden floors, a bright red leather couch, a large patterned rug, a glass coffee table and matching glass liquor cabinet, and a very large abstract painting taking up one wall. Emily caught Daniel's eye and they exchanged a glance.

"Chantelle, don't touch anything," Emily said.

Chantelle sat on the couch, her feet not reaching the floor, hands clasped in her lap, looking very intimidated by the surrounding room.

"This is insane," Emily whispered to Daniel.

They sat also, the brand new couch squeaky under their weight.

"It looked like an old money mansion from the outside," Daniel said, looking around. "But he must have had the place gutted and completely redone on the inside."

Just then, they saw Roman descending the staircase, wearing his trademark fedora.

"You made it!" he grinned, bouncing exuberantly into the room.

They stood and he skidded to a halt, arms wide for hugs. Emily felt stilted embracing Roman Westbrook. She still didn't know him very well, even though he'd gone all out by pulling some strings so they could have the fanciest hotel room on the whole of Martha's Vineyard.

"How was the honeymoon?" he asked Emily as he let her go.

"It was wonderful," Emily said.

Roman shook Daniel's hand. "And your jazz band?" he asked. "They're still doing the wedding circuit?"

"They play at the inn once a week now," Daniel confirmed.

Emily was surprised that Roman could remember so much about them. She was rather touched.

"Chantelle," Roman said, turning to the little girl. "How's my little star in the making?"

Chantelle blushed and replied shyly, "Good, thanks."

"Want to see the recording studio before dinner?" he asked.

Wide-eyed, Chantelle looked at Daniel and Emily for confirmation. They nodded.

"Okay," Chantelle said in a timid voice. It wasn't often that she was bashful these days.

Roman led his guests out of the room and into the foyer, then to a large door. He opened it to reveal a staircase heading downstairs.

"It's in the basement, of course," he said.

They all went down. It was very dark and because of the sound-canceling walls their footsteps were almost completely muffled. It was quite a strange experience, Emily thought. Like walking into the vacuum of deep space.

The recording studio was brand new, state of the art. The walls were dark and a large glass partition separated the recording area from the mixing area. There was an old-school 1940s microphone inside the recording room, a grand piano, a large double bass and a concert-sized harp. On the producer's side of the glass was the soundboard containing a million knobs and buttons and screens that indicated noise levels. Chantelle's mouth dropped open in awe.

"I'm going to speak to your school about having a choir on the background of my charity Christmas single," Roman said. "What do you think about that?"

Chantelle was too stunned to even speak.

"I think Chantelle would be very excited to sing with her choir on your Christmas single," Daniel confirmed, answering for her since she seemed too shocked to do so herself.

"Well, we can try it out after dinner," Roman said. "What do you think about that, Chantelle?"

All Chantelle could do was nod her stunned head in affirmation.

They went back upstairs and the same maid who'd greeted them at the door explained that dinner was ready to be served. Roman led them into his state-of-the-art dining room, which was all marble and glass, a stunning room of opulence. Like in the living room, there was more artwork inside, in the same abstract style of bold colors and shapes. They sat at the peculiar dining table, which was made of glass held up by a large central steel pillar.

A door opened and a chef walked in. Emily could hardly believe that Roman had his own chef-in-residence.

"I hope you're all okay with raw vegan food," Roman said.

"I can't say I've ever had it before," Emily confessed. "But I'm happy to try anything!"

The chef placed a bowl of soup in front of her. Emily wasn't sure how she felt about the prospect of raw soup. But when she took a spoonful, she was pleasantly surprised.

"It's all about using herb combinations for the flavors," Roman told them. "Different vegetables for the textures. Then sprouting seeds and beans for maximum nutrition."

"I think it's yummy," Chantelle said.

Emily just hoped she wouldn't get any ideas and start demanding similar food at home. She was certain it would be ridiculously expensive!

"This table is amazing," Emily said. "In fact, your whole style is."

"My interior designer created it," Roman said. "She's a phenomenal young woman from South Korea. Quite a talent."

"We're redesigning the house next door," Emily explained. "Opening a restaurant downstairs and adding some family-sized apartments above."

"I'll give you her details," Roman said. "Li Suh. She's delightful. I mean she's back in South Korea now but if you want to use her services she can always fly over."

Emily felt Daniel kick her under the table and she knew exactly why. There was no way they could afford to have an interior designer flown over from South Korea! Roman moved in those realms of wealth where he'd completely forgotten what normal people's lives and incomes were like. No wonder he'd been so extraordinarily generous when he paid for the drinks at the wedding and secured them the bridal suite for their honeymoon. He probably didn't even realize how lavish his gifts had been!

"How did your recording session go in LA?" Emily asked, trying to extend the same level of thoughtfulness to Roman as he had to them.

"Fabulous, thanks," Roman said. "We did a few weeks over there then we'll be doing the rest here in this studio. The album should be ready for Labor Day. Then I'll be doing a listening party for some fans. Hey, you should all come!"

"What's a listening party?" Daniel asked.

"It's when you do an intimate gig," Roman said. "I'll be playing the album in its entirety for some of my more hardcore fans. It's a way to give back, you know, considering everything they've given me." He gestured wide to encompass his whole home, his whole life, even.

"That sounds really fun," Emily said.

Chantelle was looking more excited than ever. "Can I bring Bailey?" she asked.

Roman chuckled. "Of course. It's going to be in Portland. Are you guys all right to travel?"

Emily thought of their beat-up pickup truck with a surge of embarrassment. "Sure."

"I can arrange for some cars to take you, since you're my VIPs," Roman said. "What do you say, Chantelle? Would you and your friends like to travel for a few hours in a limo? I can get a bubble machine in there. Disco lights. Sodas in an ice bucket."

Chantelle nodded, her eyes as wide as saucers.

Once again, Emily was bowled over by Roman's generosity. It almost made her feel uncomfortable to accept his offers, but she could also tell that Roman just wanted to share his wealth and treat people. So she agreed to the family attending his concert.

They finished their meal and Roman stood. “Come on, Chantelle. Let’s go and practice in the studio! I want to hear that beautiful voice of yours again.”

Chantelle didn’t need telling twice. She hurried off to the basement studio as fast as a rocket. Emily and Daniel followed with Roman, both wearing the same bewildered expression. Emily wondered if Daniel was thinking the same as she was: that Roman’s support of Chantelle might one day lead to great things.

CHAPTER EIGHT

"I think we need a date," Daniel announced to Emily that night.

They were in their bedroom, with Roman's three-course raw vegan meal still settling in their stomachs and the electrifying memory of Chantelle in a glass booth singing into the recording studio's microphone crackling through their minds.

Emily turned from her vanity mirror, midway through moisturizing, to look at Daniel lounging topless in bed. He looked gorgeous, his hair tousled just how she liked it.

"Oh?" she said with a lilt in her voice. "Are you telling me that a three-course meal at a fancy mansion doesn't count as a date?"

Daniel laughed and reached for her. "You know what I mean. We've hardly had any time to ourselves since the honeymoon. It's always chaos here. When was the last time we went out in the boat just the two of us?"

Emily stood and went over to the bed, taking Daniel's hand. He tugged her down beside him and she giggled.

"Is this about us or the boat?" she teased, knowing that Daniel had been hankering to get back out on the boat for days.

He shrugged cheekily. "Might be a bit of both," he said with a wink.

Emily laughed and smacked his bare chest. Then she sunk against him, cozying into him, feeling his breath rise and fall and the heat coming from his skin.

"That sounds like a lovely idea," she said. "Chantelle's been on at me about having a sleepover at Bailey's. I'll call Yvonne in the morning and see if she'll take her for the day."

Daniel kissed her deeply and they slid down under the covers, holding one another. Emily felt a wave of relief. Daniel had seemed distant recently but now he was very much present. When his sole focus was her, she felt like there was nothing in the world to worry about. Maybe a date would be just what she needed to quell her fears.

*

Early the next evening they dropped Chantelle at Yvonne's for a playdate with Bailey, then headed toward the harbor. Daniel carried a cooler filled with alcohol-free beers and sparkling juice, and cream cheese and watercress sandwiches he'd made himself that morning, jostling with Matthew in the kitchen for work surface space and elbow room.

Emily couldn't help but think of the other dates they'd been on, the other times they'd taken the boat out together when they'd first started seeing each other. So much had changed since then. They were married now, they had a child, and what felt like a million local friends. Even her dad had returned! She really was already making so many beautiful memories in Sunset Harbor, already had months and years behind her. It made her feel like something of an old-timer but the thought was comforting. She could hardly remember any good times back in New York City, and yet in just the short time she'd been here her life had swelled with happiness.

Taking her hand, Daniel helped her step carefully aboard the gently rocking boat. Then he began to drive them across the ocean. Emily took a deep, content breath, marveling once again at the way her life had changed and the ways in which it was to change even more once the baby was born.

"I wonder if the baby will like coming out on boat rides," Emily wondered aloud. "If he or she will like fishing as much as Chantelle."

Daniel smiled, but it looked to Emily as though the smile didn't reach his eyes. She realized then that he was preoccupied with his own thoughts once again. His mind was clearly elsewhere. She pined for that moment last night when he'd held her and made her feel like she was his whole world. What had changed, she wondered, to make him become more distant again? The mention of the baby? Emily could tell there was still something he was holding back, but she didn't want to ruin their date by prying. She decided that today at least she was going to just let it go.

They took a new route this time, a longer journey in order to take in the whole of the sunset. The sky was a beautiful burst of pink, with orange streaks and puffy purple clouds, the sun a golden orb that sunk toward the horizon.

"Hey, look over there," Daniel said, pointing across the sparkling waves. "I've never seen that island before."

Emily squinted into the distance, taking in the sight of the land mass ahead of them. "I thought you'd explored every inch of the Maine coast," she said.

Daniel smirked. "Do you have any idea how many islands there are in these waters? Thousands. Some *have* escaped my notice." He chuckled. "So, can we stop there?" he asked.

He seemed excited and Emily wanted him to stay happy.

"Of course," she said with a shrug. "Looks as good a place as any."

Daniel set their course for the direction of the island and the boat sliced through the waves toward it. When they reached the rocky land, Daniel secured the boat and they both clambered out.

The beach was mainly shell and rock, overgrown by brush, giving it a wild and romantic feel. Just off the beach was a dense forest of spruce trees. Red squirrels scurried up their trunks.

Looking around, Emily saw there were signs of the remnants of an old fishing village, crude shacks and abandoned lobster trawlers.

"This is amazing," she said, feeling awed by the island. It felt like a relic of a time gone by. "I wonder when people quit living here."

"It looks like a really small island," Daniel said. "A couple of acres at most. It was probably just an outpost for the fishing community, rather than a place anyone actually lived."

They strolled around, hand in hand. It didn't take them long to cover the whole island. Emily was charmed by its tranquility, its ruggedness.

"We'll have to bring Chantelle back here some time," she said. "I bet she'd love it. And the new baby."

"Maybe when it's older," Daniel replied. "I don't know how much I'd like to have a baby all the way out here. It's pretty barren."

It was a good point, and it made Emily glad to hear him thinking protectively over their child. He may not seem as thrilled about it as she was, but he certainly had a father's mentality about the whole thing.

"Look at this sign, Daniel," Emily said, spotting a wooden post with a faded rectangular board nailed to it. "The island is for sale!"

She couldn't believe it as she looked at the price for the two acre piece of land. "Forty thousand dollars. That can't be right," she said. "They must be missing a zero or two."

Daniel looked surprised as well. "Maybe smaller islands like this sell for less. If you think about it, two acres is less ground than our lawn." He peered closer at the sign. "Look, it says the water comes from a well. No electricity or Internet. I guess that's why."

Emily still couldn't believe it. Even without running water the price seemed like a steal!

"Can you imagine if we bought an island?" she said with a laugh. "Everyone would think we were crazy."

"We *would* be crazy," Daniel confirmed. Then his eyes sparkled with imagination. "Although, how awesome would it be if we turned it into an adventure playground for Chantelle!"

Knowing Daniel, Emily knew that such a feat was within his grasp. If he could make a baby's crib and a spiral wooden staircase he could certainly construct some monkey bars and a treetop trail.

It delighted Emily to see his more playful side coming back out, and so she joined in.

"We could make it into an exotic animal sanctuary," she suggested. "Alpacas. Or, actually, we could turn it into one of those islands you get in Japan that are overrun with bunnies!"

Daniel laughed. "*Or*," he said," his expression more serious now, "it could be an offshoot of the inn."

Emily smiled but frowned at the same time. "I was only joking," she said. "We're not really going to buy an island!"

"Why not?" Daniel said, and he seemed suddenly genuine. "It's not like we can't afford it."

It was a good point but Emily shook her head. "No one would want to stay here without water and electricity."

"Sure they would," Daniel said, his expression turning more and more excited. "Especially if we filled it with yurts and made it a luxury camping experience."

Emily's eyes widened then. Daniel was actually being serious. He wasn't quite suggesting they call the real estate agent up immediately, but he was certainly suggesting they consider it.

Could they do it? Open a camping offshoot to the inn? Her mind started to race with possibilities.

"We could build a jetty here," Daniel continued, indicating a flat spot on the otherwise rocky beach. "People could row themselves over, or we could hire someone to do it for them. We could have some docks as well for people who want to moor. Buy some yachts that we could rent out for explorer types."

Emily saw the glitter in Daniel's eyes and admired his ambition. She wondered what had made him dream so grandly recently, and hoped it was something to do with him wanting to provide for their growing family.

"We could definitely consider it for the future," she said. "We have so much happening at the moment with Trevor's expansion, though, I don't know if Doctor Arkwright would be happy with me if I told her I was also converting an island! Plus, I'm just not sure how to monetize it. We know nothing about opening a campsite. Is there really a demand for camping on an island with no running water? We'd have to do some research."

Daniel laughed and his overexuberance calmed down. "Good point. But can we please keep it in mind?"

Though intrigued by the idea, Emily just wasn't convinced that they could make it work. There was so much happening as it was, the last thing they needed was more homework, more bank meetings, more drawing up business plans. Still, she was always happy when Daniel was focused and excited about something so she didn't want to dash his spirits.

"I guess," she replied, finally.

They settled down on the beach and opened up the picnic. They had a bottle of alcohol-free beer each, and clinked the rims in celebration of finally having made it out on a date with just the two of them. As they sipped together, side by side, looking out at the ocean where the last rays of golden sunshine were extinguished by the horizon, Emily felt like everything was right in the world.

CHAPTER NINE

6 WEEKS LATER

The sun had barely started rising when Emily jolted upright in bed. The now familiar sensation of nausea washed over her. She leapt up and rushed into the en suite bathroom, just making it to the toilet in time. She sunk to her knees and heaved.

The sound of footsteps came behind her and she knew that Daniel had been awoken by the noise. She felt his hands upon her back, rubbing her gently as she continued throwing up.

"Happy Fourth of July," she heard him say.

Between gags, Emily could only manage a grunting noise of agreement.

She'd just reached the fourteenth week of pregnancy, the second trimester when everything was supposed to settle down, but her symptoms were worse than ever. The first trimester had been a piece of cake in comparison to now.

"Your morning sickness seems to be getting worse," Daniel said gently, as his hand moved in circular motions between her shoulder blades.

Her heaving subsided and she sat back against the tiled floor. She rested her back against the wall and panted. Daniel handed her a glass of water.

"Thank you," she murmured, taking the smallest sip.

Daniel swept the flyaway hairs from her face, smoothing them back behind her ears. Emily knew she must look a mess. In some ways she wished Daniel didn't have to see her like this. In other ways she was desperately grateful for his support. Throwing up every morning alone would be awful.

"Think you're done?" Daniel asked.

Emily touched her abdomen to see whether the pressure would cause another wave of nausea. It did not. She nodded.

Daniel helped her to her feet. Right in the middle of the bathroom they embraced, him holding her closely against her chest. Emily felt so comfortable and cared for when they stood like this.

"Sorry for waking you up so early," Emily said.

Then Daniel released her from his protective arms. "It's fine. I wanted to get an early start on the spa today anyway. We should probably head down for breakfast," he said.

"Do you have to work today?" Emily said. "It's the Fourth of July. Can't we just spend the time together?"

Emily knew he was only next door but there were times when her pregnancy left her feeling vulnerable and wanting him next to her. Daniel was so busy at the moment, with work at Jack's and the additional time spent on the spa renovation she felt like she barely ever saw him anymore. Some days she would head up to bed alone, and only see him in the morning when she awoke to see him sleeping deeply beside her. He was exhausting himself with work and it worried her, since once the baby arrived they probably wouldn't get a full night's sleep for at least a year!

Daniel cupped her face in his hands. "We'll be spending the whole time together tonight at the party. And you know we're on a tight schedule. I want to get the work done in the outhouse as quickly as possible. I'm sorry. Will you be okay?"

Emily nodded. She still felt clammy all over from the sickness but knew the worst of it had now passed.

"It's just next door," Daniel added in a reassuring tone. "If you need me don't hesitate to come over."

While missing Daniel on one hand, Emily was also very glad that they'd decided on Daniel doing as much of the woodworking renovation as possible, because having him nearby was very reassuring on days such as these where she felt awful and completely wiped out.

Daniel massaged her shoulders as she brushed her teeth and washed her face with cool water.

"Let's get out of this damn bathroom," Emily said once she was done. "I swear I've seen the inside of that toilet bowl enough to last me for a lifetime."

Daniel supported her as they walked out the room and down the stairs. As they passed through the foyer, Lois waved to get Emily's attention.

“A call came in last night from Wesley,” Lois said, beaming from ear to ear. “Suzanna gave birth to a healthy baby boy at two in the morning. They’re calling him Robin.”

Emily squealed with delight. It thrilled her to know that her own unborn baby had a ready-made playmate in Suzanna and Wesley’s precious new son. She’d have to send a gift to her friends, get Chantelle to create one of her infamous gift baskets.

Emily and Daniel headed onward to the kitchen and saw that Chantelle was already awake and sitting at the breakfast bar, a coloring book spread open in front of her. She’d dressed herself in pink dungarees.

“How are you feeling today, Mommy?” she asked.

“Awful,” Emily said. Then she smiled. “But thanks for asking. Did Lois tell you the exciting news?”

Chantelle’s eyes widened. She shook her head.

“Toby’s baby brother was born during the night!” Emily told her. “They named him Robin.”

Chantelle looked delighted. “Fourth of July birthday,” she exclaimed. “He’s so lucky. It means he’ll always be surrounded by friends and family every year.”

Emily nodded as Daniel helped her onto a stool. “Do you want to make them a gift basket?”

Chantelle nodded eagerly.

“What do you want for breakfast?” Daniel asked Emily.

The thought of food made Emily’s stomach turn again. “Just some plain toast,” she said.

“That’s all? What about juice?”

She shook her head. The thought of orange juice disgusted her.

Daniel looked worried as he made her two pieces of plain toast. Even Chantelle looked concerned. Emily was just glad that they were both so loving and caring as to worry about her. Other than the sickness, she felt fine, and she was glad that the light-headedness Doctor Arkwright had warned her of had not come to fruition.

“I’d better go,” Daniel said, handing her the plate of toast. “There’s so much to get done. Will you be okay?”

Emily nodded and took the plate from him. “I’ll be fine. I’ve got my special helper here.” She smiled at Chantelle.

Daniel ruffled the child’s hair. “Take good care of Mommy. I’m just right next door if you need me.”

He left quickly, in a blur. Emily heard the sound of the front door clicking shut then began to eat her breakfast in the smallest bites imaginable.

"Did Matthew make you anything for breakfast this morning?" Emily asked Chantelle.

The little girl put down her pink pen and looked up. She nodded.

"I had cereal," she said.

There was a despondency in her tone, Emily noted. Something was wrong.

"Honey, you don't need to worry about me," she said. "It's completely normal to be sick when you're pregnant."

"It's not that," Chantelle replied. She turned her attention back down to the elephant in her coloring book and carried on turning it pink.

"What is it?" Emily asked softly, wondering if Suzanna and Wesley's news had stirred some latent fears to surface in the child. "You know you can tell me anything."

Chantelle chewed her lip. Then she said, "It's just that I prayed every night for Papa Roy to FaceTime us and he never did."

Emily felt terrible for the child. She hadn't yet had a chance to get used to being disappointed by Roy in the same way Emily had. Chantelle hadn't been let down by him yet; this was the first time. It must be bitterly upsetting for her.

And Emily herself was worried about her father. She hadn't received a response to the letter she'd sent, and wondered whether it had gotten lost in the mail. Or maybe Roy had read the news of her pregnancy and freaked out. Maybe he was out of touch again? Maybe something had happened to him? The more she thought about it, the more upset she felt. But she couldn't let Chantelle see her worry, so she smiled.

"Papa Roy still doesn't have a phone," she explained. "And it takes a really long time for letters to reach England. They have to cross the ocean, after all."

"But are we still going to have a vacation with him?" Chantelle asked, looking perturbed.

"Of course!" Emily said brightly, though she wasn't sure herself and was in fact rather worried that the promised vacation wouldn't happen at all.

Chantelle didn't look convinced either. Emily decided that she needed a distraction.

"Are you excited about the Fourth of July celebrations tonight?" she asked. "We're having a big party at the inn."

"I forgot!" Chantelle exclaimed. "I still need to put up my decorations. It's going to be sparkly stars this year and shiny streamers."

"Sounds wonderful," Emily said. Chantelle's creative decorations of the inn were one of her favorite things. "When do you want to start?"

"Later," Chantelle said with a shrug. She went back to her coloring.

Emily realized that the distraction technique had not worked. She thought more creatively.

"I was thinking of fixing up the baby's room today. Do you want to help?"

This time, Chantelle couldn't contain her excitement. She dropped her pen, immediately done with coloring the elephant on her page though it was only halfway completed.

"Yes, yes, yes!" she cried.

Emily beamed. "Come on then. Let's get started."

They went upstairs and along the hall to the room they'd decided would be changed from a guest room to the new baby's nursery. Daniel had already moved the furniture out, selling some to Rico and repurposing other bits at Jack Cooper's to sell in the future. Inside there were now only two things; Amy's Scandinavian-style nursing chair, and Daniel's hand-crafted crib.

"Daddy made this," Emily told Chantelle. "Look." She pushed it and the cribbed rocked back and forth.

"That's clever," Chantelle said, beaming with pride.

They got to work stripping the wallpaper and pulling up the carpet. Emily had decided to get a charcoal shag rug to match the nursing stool and to put in a cream-colored carpet beneath it. She didn't want the room to echo and risk having her crying baby wake up the guests!

Removing the wallpaper was a tedious job and Emily half wished she'd hired someone else to do it. But she also thought it was a good bonding exercise for her and Chantelle, and Daniel when he had the time. This way it felt like they were all involved with the baby, and would all get a sense of accomplishment.

Chantelle was busy scratching paper off the wall with a putty knife. She was wearing a very serious expression as she worked.

Emily smiled to herself, proud of how mature Chantelle had become recently.

"Do you think Sheila will have had her baby by now?" Chantelle asked Emily.

There it was, Emily thought, the surfacing of Chantelle's concerns that she'd worried about. Suzanna's baby news must have reminded the little girl of Sheila's pregnancy because she'd learned about them both during the same period of time.

But Emily wasn't sure what to tell her. Because Chantelle had never shown her the content of Sheila's letter all those months ago there was no way of knowing for sure how far along she'd been when she'd broken the news initially. She'd sported a neat bump at the adoption proceedings, which could have indicated anything from a large four-month to a small six-month. If it had been closer to six months, it was certainly likely that she'd had the child by now.

"She might have," Emily said. "If not, it will be very soon."

Chantelle nodded and went back to scraping.

"How do you feel about that?" Emily asked, cautiously.

"I don't know," Chantelle confessed. "I thought I would feel sad. But now I have a different baby brother or sister on the way so I don't think I really mind. It's not like I want to be Sheila's daughter anymore anyway so there's no way I'd get to play with her baby."

Emily was glad that Chantelle could take such a mature attitude to the whole thing, though she hoped Chantelle might soften as she grew older about cutting Sheila out of her life completely. Emily knew that family relationships could be strained, trying, and damaging at times, but she still kept minimal contact with her own mother because she knew she'd feel significantly worse if she didn't. They had until Chantelle reached eleven before anything would happen with regards to her having contact with Sheila, so there was plenty of time for Chantelle to digest the situation and change her mind.

Just then, Emily heard some banging noises coming from outside. She looked out the window and saw that several work vans had arrived next door while they'd been working on the nursery, and were now unloading crates of goods into Trevor's house. There were also several people with huge spades in Trevor's yard.

"Come and look, Chantelle," she called to the girl. "They're starting the landscaping work."

Chantelle rushed over to the window and watched with bated breath as the diggers took down the fences between the two houses, effectively doubling the size of the inn's grounds.

They watched together as the fence came down completely, along with the large trees that Trevor had planted years ago to stop his neighbors snooping on him. Then the diggers started bringing up mounds of soil, landscaping the garden in preparation for Raj's final work. As they watched, Emily noticed the crew stop and crowd around something.

"What are they doing?" Chantelle asked.

"It looks like they've found something in the dirt," she said.

One of the crew turned then and looked up at the window where they were standing. He waved them down.

"I wonder what it could be," Emily said, filled with intrigue, as she and Chantelle left the room.

They trotted down the stairs and out onto the lawns, then hurried across to the crew. When they got there, they saw Daniel exiting the outhouse as well, approaching the crowd with a curious expression.

"What have you found?" Emily asked the workman who was standing in a large hole.

He looked up. "It's a tin box," he said. He managed to wedge it out of the soil and handed it up to Emily.

She took the tin in her hands, turning it over. It was rather large, perhaps an old cookie assortment tin. As she wiped the dirt from it, she recognized the faded design beneath, of a Victorian lady sharing a cup of tea with friends at a bistro table. The tin had been Roy's, one of a myriad amongst his collection of trinkets. As she regarded it, a memory was sparked in her mind, of her father giving her and Charlotte the tin one day. But that was as much as her mind could recall.

"Is it a time capsule?" she said with a gasp, shaking it gently and hearing it rattle. She felt a surge of emotion as she tried to prize open the lid with her fingertips only to discover it was stuck fast.

"Here," Daniel said, gesturing for it.

She handed it to him.

"Careful," she said. "Don't damage it."

Daniel tried, too, to open the tin but it was stuck. "Let's go inside and use something to pry it open."

They all went inside the inn and into the living room. Chantelle watched with excitement as Daniel fetched his flat-head screwdriver from his toolbox and began to prize the lid open.

Finally it popped off and clattered to the floor. Emily winced. Daniel looked up at Emily with a grimace. "Sorry."

Chantelle grabbed the lid. "It's okay. Not damaged or anything." She handed it to Emily.

"So?" Emily asked Daniel. She bit her lip, feeling apprehensive at the thought of seeing what was inside.

"You were right," he confirmed with the nod of his head. "It looks like a time capsule."

He held it up to Emily.

She took it in her hands delicately, cradling it, knowing that there was only one person who could have buried it: Charlotte. Memories returned to her as she looked at all the little items inside, some damaged by water, but most remarkably intact. Small plastic toys, trading cards, and drawings. Emily saw a handwritten note and pulled it out. She recognized Charlotte's childish scrawl instantly.

When I grow up I want to be a doctor. I want to live in a house by the beach like my daddy, but in a lighthouse, not a normal house, and my big sister Emily can live there too. We'll have five cats and a turtle. There will be chickens in the garden so we can eat eggs every day.

Tears sprung into Emily's eyes. She folded the paper away, holding it against her heart.

"What did it say, Mommy?" Chantelle asked.

Emily looked tearfully at the child, her mind conjuring the image of Charlotte in her face more strongly than ever. "It's a letter my little sister wrote about what she wanted to do when she grew up." A tear trickled down her cheek. "But she never got to grow up."

Chantelle touched her arm lightly. "Why don't you tell me and Daddy about her? That's what Gail says to do, when you miss people. To think of some happy memories about them. That way they don't feel so far away."

Emily smiled, touched by Chantelle's words, by the fact she wanted to cheer Emily up and take away her tears. "Okay," Emily began. "Charlotte loved animals. And drawing. She was very creative. She loved to party, to decorate the house and make cards."

As Emily spoke, she realized how she could just as readily be describing Chantelle. The similarities between her sister and the young girl were striking, almost eerie.

"What animal was her favorite?" Chantelle asked, her expression conveying to Emily genuine interest in Charlotte. It occurred to Emily then that she'd never really spoken at length about Charlotte to Chantelle. But the child was clearly curious about the aunt she'd never get to know.

"Well, she loved dogs," Emily said, think of Persephone, Toni's golden Labrador that Charlotte had adored. "But I don't know if they were her favorite animal."

Chantelle looked up at Emily with her big blue eyes, something glittering behind them that made her look suddenly older than her years. "I wonder if it was turtles," she said. "Or cats?"

Emily's breath caught. She glanced briefly at Charlotte's letter, at the mention of turtles and cats. She herself had no memory of Charlotte being fond of turtles or cats so there was no way she'd mentioned it in passing. Chantelle must have made a lucky guess, she told herself in an attempt to quell the spooky sensation tingling up her spine.

"Maybe," Emily said, her voice thinning.

"What else was she like?" Chantelle quizzed Emily.

"I don't remember too well anymore," Emily explained, feeling a little sad at the fading memories, at the ones lost forever. "She had a wonderful imagination. She liked to dress up and play make-believe games."

"Like pirates?" Chantelle asked. "Hunting for treasure?"

A jolt hit Emily then as she recalled the treasure chest she'd found in the attic when she'd first come to the house. It had sparked a memory in her of the imaginative games the two had played together in their youth. Chantelle must have found the treasure chest, Emily told herself sternly. There was no other explanation for it… was there?

The tingles in her spine grew stronger and stronger. She'd felt Charlotte's presence in the house before, her spirit watching over. Was she here now?

She looked at Daniel. He seemed to be in his own world, completely occupied with work-related documents, forms, and letters that he was studying intently. He wasn't paying any attention to them at all. It was as if Emily and Chantelle were existing within a protective bubble, just the two of them, the outside world fading to nothing.

"Yes," Emily replied. Her voice was becoming a whisper. "Like pirates."

She looked into Chantelle's eyes and saw that same flicker behind them; of knowing, of deeper understanding. Was it Charlotte?

"Following treasure maps," Chantelle said. "Steering the boat through storms at sea."

Emily could hardly catch her breath. Chantelle wasn't asking questions anymore. It felt more like she was telling Emily how it was, like she was recalling a memory rather than guessing at one.

"A stuffed parrot companion," Chantelle continued. "Peg legs made of wood."

As she spoke, it felt as if she was adding to Emily's memories, bringing to the forefront things she had forgotten. The stuffed toy bird they would wrestle over—not a parrot but a toucan, though it was the closest thing they had available. And peg legs they would try and fail to tie to their knees, usually dissolving in laughter at their attempts to walk.

A chill swept through Emily's entire body. "Maybe we should put this away," she said, motioning to put the lid back on the tin. She was getting too freaked out.

"But we've hardly looked inside yet," Chantelle said.

Emily faltered. She couldn't be certain whether Charlotte's spirit was with them but she could definitely feel something, and it compelled her to continue looking through the contents of the tin.

There were more toys, some cassette tapes, a wilted daisy chain that disintegrated when Emily touched it. Then she found more paper. Another letter. She opened it up.

This is the first box but not the last box. If you want to find the next one you will need to swim!

Emily frowned and handed it to Chantelle. "It's a riddle," she said, thinking instantly of their father. This was just like him. Had Charlotte been inspired by Roy? Or helped by him to lay a treasure hunt of time capsules? "A clue to another box."

"How exciting!" Chantelle exclaimed.

Emily looked at her and saw the child once again, not Charlotte, nor that knowing look that had lingered behind her eyes. She just looked like an exuberant kid, excited at the prospect of a time capsule treasure hunt. Even Daniel, sitting on the couch, seemed to have suddenly returned to the present. The eerie moment was over, leaving Emily with a strange feeling in her chest.

"Do you think there's another box at the beach?" Chantelle asked Emily. "That's where people swim."

Emily shrugged. "I have no idea. But if it is, there's a chance we won't ever find it. The beach is very big."

"We can't give up!" Chantelle exclaimed. "We'll buy a metal detector to help us search the beach."

Emily loved the girl's enthusiasm for the project, but felt in her heart that they would never find the next capsule. The clue could easily be directing them to one of the islands off the coast of Maine, and Daniel had told her there were thousands of them. They'd never find it!

"That's a lovely idea," Emily said, agreeing with Chantelle. She didn't want to dash her hopes. Plus, it warmed her heart to know that her daughter cared so much about Charlotte.

They put everything back in the tin. It had been a wonderful discovery and Emily knew she would treasure it forever, even if they never found the next capsule. But her heart felt heavy at the same time. Feeling Charlotte's spirit had unsettled her, and looking through the tin that she'd once so diligently filled made her absence feel suddenly bigger.

Just then, she felt Chantelle's arms wrap around her waist. She hugged the girl, feeling comforted by her presence, consoled by her.

"I think Mommy needs cheering up," Chantelle whispered loudly to Daniel.

He was watching them patiently. Emily looked at him and smiled her pride at how caring and sweet their daughter was.

"What do you think we should do to cheer Mommy up?" Daniel replied in an equally loud whisper.

"I think there's supposed to be a fair down on the beach for the Fourth of July," Chantelle said. "We could go and see what it's like. Yvonne said she would be there."

"I think that's a very good idea," Daniel said. "Why don't you ask Mommy?"

Emily pretended she hadn't heard a word of their whispered conversation when Chantelle drew out of the hug and announced, "Mommy, I have an idea."

"What's that?" Emily asked, feigned curiosity in her tone.

"I think we should all go down to the beach for the Fourth of July celebration. We can collect shells and eat cotton candy. Bailey said there's a face painter there too. Do you want your face painted?"

Emily smiled, comforted by her sweet daughter. She squeezed her. "I'd love to."

Chantelle didn't need any more encouragement. She tugged Emily's hand and began leading her toward the door. Emily laughed and shook her head. Daniel followed, looking as equally touched and amused as Emily felt.

CHAPTER TEN

The beach was crowded with families, groups of young people dressed in patriotic colors, and hordes of children. It was gloriously sunny and everyone ran around in high spirits. It seemed to Emily that everywhere she looked there was another woman pushing a newborn in a stroller or cradling one in their arms.

Stalls lined the perimeter of the beach, mainly geared up for the children. There was a Frisbee-making stall where Chantelle got to squirt red, white, and blue paint into a spinning machine. She also visited the face painter, who gave her a sparkly red star on her cheek, and the lady in the temporary tattoo stall where she chose a red bow for her forearm.

"Look, an ice cream truck!" Chantelle cried excitedly.

She dragged her parents over and spent a dollar on a cherry-flavored sno-cone. Emily got herself a creamy vanilla cone and Daniel a mint chocolate chip one. Then they sat on a picnic bench and ate happily.

"I wish there was always ice cream and stalls on the beach," Chantelle said. "Not just on the Fourth of July."

"We'd probably spend more time here if there was," Emily said, surprised herself that they rarely used the beach when it was just across the street from them.

Emily noticed her friend Yvonne approaching with her daughter, Bailey, who was Chantelle's best friend. Chantelle leapt up and hugged Bailey and then proceeded to show off her tattoo and face paint proudly.

"Did you hear about baby Robin?" Yvonne asked, hugging Emily.

"I did. It's so exciting! I'm thrilled for them."

Emily felt her own secret on the tip of her tongue. How easy it would be to let her friend know she was also expecting. But she managed to hold it in.

"This is great, isn't it?" Yvonne said, looking around at the fun beach event. "They should put this on every year. It's better for the kids than a parade."

"I'll send a petition to Mayor Hansen," Emily joked. "No more parades. Beach parties only from now on, thank you very much."

Everyone laughed.

Yvonne joined them for an ice cream, then they were shortly followed by more parents from school. Everyone was buzzing about the news of Suzanna and Wesley's new baby, the excitement palpable in the air. It gave the already buoyant celebrations an even more exuberant atmosphere.

It seemed to Emily like everyone she'd ever met in Sunset Harbor had congregated on the beach for the day. As she looked around, Emily was surprised by just how many people they now knew. Chantelle's circle of friends seemed to grow day by day, and with it the number of parents that Emily and Daniel got to become friends with. The thought pleased her immensely.

The children got to work building a sandcastle, giving the adults some downtime to sit and chat about actual grown-up things. But Emily couldn't help find her mind wandering to Suzanna's baby news, and her attention drawn to the table next to her, where there was a group of four young moms with babies of various ages shrieking in a variety of pitches and levels of distress.

Emily watched on as the mothers attempted to find out what was the matter with their children, from checking on their diaper situations to giving them pacifiers, rocking them, winding them, rattling toys in their faces. All the while the infants shrieked and wailed. It all looked very stressful. Emily couldn't believe she would be one of those mothers soon. The thought started to panic her. Did she have that kind of patience? What if she had a child that always cried, that was never soothed? How would she cope?

"Emily, what's wrong?" Daniel asked, concerned.

Emily tore her gaze from the table of new mothers and looked at Daniel, her expression panic-stricken. She hoped none of the others at the table had noticed her freak-out. She still wasn't quite ready to reveal to her friends that she was pregnant. She wanted some kind of acknowledgment from her father before she revealed it to the rest of the world.

"Babies," she whispered under her breath.

She looked over her shoulder and Daniel followed her gaze. When she turned back to him he was smiling.

"It's not funny," she stammered. "Look how stressed they all are. They look overwhelmed."

Daniel carried on smiling. “Emily, it’s going to be okay. Honestly. Babies cry. Parents make mistakes.”

“But I don’t know if I can do that,” Emily replied. She could hear her voice becoming more shrill.

“Of course you can,” Daniel said simply.

“I won’t be able to keep my composure if my baby is screaming like that in public!”

Daniel rubbed her arm. “Yes, you will,” he reassured her. “You’re going to be an amazing mom. You already are.” He gestured to where Chantelle was laughing with her friends on the beach beside the huge, elaborate sandcastle they’d constructed together.

Emily wanted to be reassured by Daniel’s words but she herself wasn’t so sure. Chantelle had come to them fully formed, a child with interests. They could play with her, reason with her, have conversations with her. They’d never had to change her diaper or feed her in the middle of the night. They’d never had to deal with her spit-up or colic. It was all that stuff that seemed suddenly daunting to Emily. Daniel may have faith in her ability to cope with it all.

But Emily wasn’t certain she had faith in herself.

*

Emily’s anxiety didn’t abate that day. Even while watching the inn’s firework display on the porch with all the staff and guests, all she could think about was her appointment with Doctor Arkwright tomorrow. They were due to find out the gender. She should be excited, but instead she was filled with worry. What if it was a boy? Boys were supposed to be rambunctious and accident prone. But then again baby girls were supposed to cry more and express greater anxiety. Then a thought of utter horror struck her. What if she was having twins?

Emily couldn’t stop herself from mulling these thoughts over and over in her mind, speculating what her life would be like once the baby arrived.

“Did you know that Mommy gets to see the baby tomorrow?” Daniel asked Chantelle.

It was as if he’d read Emily’s mind. She leaned against the porch post, her arms tightening around her for comfort. Behind them, the sky exploded with blue sparkles.

"How?" Chantelle asked, perplexed.

"There's a machine," Daniel explained. "It can look inside the body, a bit like an X-ray. The doctor will tell us whether you're having a brother or sister."

He touched Emily's stomach as he spoke. As though in response her heart fluttered with anxiety. She felt on the periphery of their conversation rather than a part of it.

"I want a sister," Chantelle said. "What about you, Daddy?"

"Well, I already have the best daughter in the world," he said, ruffling her hair. "So I think I'd prefer it to be a boy."

They both looked up at Emily then, expectantly. She shifted from one foot to the other feeling suddenly put on the spot.

"What about you, Mommy?" Chantelle asked when Emily stayed quiet.

"I don't mind either way," Emily said. "As long as it's healthy. And not twins."

Chantelle's eyes widened. "Twins? I hadn't thought of that!"

Daniel shook his head and laughed. "It won't be twins."

He stroked Emily's arm tenderly but it didn't help resolve her worry. She always felt like they were at odds with one another. When Daniel wanted kids, she didn't. Whenever she felt excited about the baby, he seemed stressed. And now they'd switched again. He was relaxed about finding out the baby's sex in their appointment tomorrow whereas it had prompted an anxiety attack in her. She wished they could get into sync with one another.

An enormous *boom* sounded in the sky, followed by fizzling sparkly lights. Like Daniel and Chantelle, the gathered guests made appreciative noises, their eyes turned to the sky, their expressions joyful. Emily wanted to enjoy this moment, to put her fears to rest. She took a deep breath in an attempt to calm herself.

"Why don't we do a gender reveal party?" Daniel suddenly suggested.

Chantelle tore her eyes away from the display momentarily in order to exclaim, "Party!"

Emily was shocked. She frowned in Daniel's direction.

"Really?" she asked, the surprise audible in her tone. She couldn't help but feel like gender parties were a little on the twee side, the sort of thing her New York City friends would do in order to show off and get more attention. She hated all forms of attention. The wedding had been plenty for her. And for the suggestion to have come from Daniel—who was usually very logical and practical about things—made it even more surprising.

She thought about his reasoning for a moment and wondered if this was spurred on, once again, by how much he'd missed out on with Chantelle. Maybe he wanted to make sure he got to experience everything this time, from the gender parties to the baby shower. It just felt so strange.

"You don't think it's a good idea?" Daniel asked in response to her prolonged silence.

"It's not that," Emily said with a shrug. "It just feels a bit … showy. Extravagant."

There was a pause in the explosion of fireworks and Chantelle turned then, looking up at Emily, bemused. "You love parties," she stated. "We both do."

"I know, I know," Emily replied, rubbing her forehead. She couldn't quite put into words her reticence so decided it would probably be better to just relent. It was a two against one situation anyway so she was going to lose either way. "We'll do a gender reveal if it's what you both want."

"Yay!" Chantelle exclaimed. "How do we do it?"

Daniel explained. "What we do is get Doctor Arkwright to put the gender in an envelope without telling us. Then we can give it to Karen to bake into a cake—pink for a girl, blue for a boy. Then when we cut open the cake we'll be surprised along with everyone else."

Emily chewed her lip. "That would mean Karen finds out before other people."

"That's okay, isn't it?" Daniel said. "Karen *is* your friend."

"Yes, but wouldn't it be a bit strange? Her knowing before us? Especially when no one even knows I'm pregnant yet! What if she accidentally told someone else? I'd feel more comfortable if it were made by someone who didn't know us at all."

"You are peculiar," Daniel said, planting a kiss on her forehead. "But we can go to another bakery and get it done there if you prefer."

Emily nodded, a little relieved. She tried to analyze where her reticence was coming from and realized that it wasn't really that she didn't want Karen finding out the gender first, but that she didn't feel ready yet to let people know she was pregnant at all.

"Are we having the party tomorrow then?" Chantelle asked. "After the doctor?"

Emily felt her face blanch. "That means everyone will know I'm pregnant… The whole town. My staff. All our friends."

Chantelle's eyes sparkled at the realization that the time had finally come to spill the Morey family secret. But then a new emotion passed through them, one that Emily recognized to be grief.

"But Papa Roy…" Chantelle said quietly. "We still don't know if he knows. It wouldn't be right to tell anyone before him, would it?"

Emily rubbed her back gently. She realized that she felt the same way, that that had been why she'd felt such anxiety about revealing the news. She felt Daniel's hand touch her arm gently.

"We can wait a little longer if you want," he said. "There's no rush."

Emily paused for a moment and thought it through. But she had to accept that she couldn't put off telling people forever. She couldn't put her life on hold because of her father again.

"I think it's time we stopped waiting," she said.

"Then it's tomorrow?" Daniel asked.

"Tomorrow," Emily confirmed.

Chantelle nodded too, then her slightly sad expression was replaced by a mischievous smile that appeared on her lips.

"I don't think you should tell anyone what the party is for," she said. "It should be a baby reveal. Then a surprise gender reveal. That way it's extra surprising."

Emily smiled too. "I love that idea." She looked at Daniel. "What do you say?"

His eyes twinkled with the same mischief as his daughter. Then he nodded.

"Let's do it."

CHAPTER ELEVEN

Emily found herself more nervous than ever as she, Daniel, and Chantelle entered Doctor Arkwright's office.

"Lie down here for me," Doctor Arkwright said.

Emily got onto the table and pulled her top up so that Doctor Arkwright could apply the cool jelly substance. Then she used the ultrasound machine's wand, moving it around Emily's stomach. With bated breath, Emily watched the monitor.

Chantelle seemed to buzz with excitement.

"Okay, so that's the heartbeat there," Doctor Arkwright said, pointing at a small flickering black blob on the screen. "Baby is lying at the top here, so if I just angle this way." She moved the machine across Emily's stomach. All at once, the unmistakable shape of a baby came into view. "There we go," Doctor Arkwright finished. "That's the spine. Head."

Chantelle squealed with delight. Daniel's eyes opened wider. Emily thought she saw tears welling in them. She herself felt overwhelmed with emotion.

"Now, you're all going to want to close your eyes now," Doctor Arkwright said. "So I can have a peek and see what the sex is."

Emily averted her gaze from the monitor, her heart fluttering as Doctor Arkwright moved the machine around. In her mind's eye she could still see the monitor, the image of her baby, their baby. It was unreal. Amazing. She felt a surge of joy rush through her.

"Okay, all done," Doctor Arkwright said. "I'll write it down and put it in a sealed envelope. Along with the sonogram picture because I don't want you guessing by looking too closely."

She chuckled and scribbled something down on a piece of paper. Then she slipped it in an envelope, sealed it shut, and handed it to Chantelle.

"I think it will be safest with you," she said, smiling.

Chantelle took the envelope, looking proud and important as she clutched it in her hands. Emily smiled at her happily, feeling content and excited.

She sat up and wiped her belly clean.

"Next stop, the cake shop," she said.

Suddenly, the idea of a reveal party seemed like the most exciting thing in the world. It was just a shame her father wasn't going to be there—not even through FaceTime—to enjoy the moment with them. The thought saddened her. It was just another moment he had missed out on in her life. But she was determined to not let it spoil her happiness.

*

After dropping the instructions for the cake to the baker in the next town over, the family returned home and began planning the party. Chantelle, of course, took command, and Emily was very happy to let her. It pleased her to see the child getting so involved in everything. That Chantelle gave her blessing to the baby meant the world to Emily.

"How do we know what colors to decorate?" Chantelle said, as they sat together at the kitchen table to plan. Her notebook was spread open in front of her, her trusty pink sparkly pen in her hand.

"We could go for neutral colors," Daniel said. "White. Green. That sort of thing."

Chantelle looked horrified. "A *green* gender reveal? You're not having an alien!"

Emily laughed. "We'll have to split it, half and half. How about we have pink and blue balloons, then everyone can pop the ones we don't need once we find out?"

"And we could have pink and blue streamers, but only pop the colors we need," Chantelle added, looking really excited. "That way, once we find out, the decorations will change to the right ones."

"That's a great idea," Daniel said. "How about paper chains across the ceiling too? We could make blue ones and pink ones and have a person in each corner of the room so that when the gender is revealed, they pull on the correct chain and stick it in the corner."

"I love this idea," Emily said, imagining in her mind the room suddenly turning blue around her, or pink.

They went into the living room and Chantelle created a sign that said SORRY - THIS ROOM IS CURRENTLY UNAVAILABLE FOR GUESTS. They then got to work, making long paper chains that could stretch across the length of the large living room. Daniel fixed them into place in the corners of the room, and they decided that the four volunteers who would fix them in place should be Keiran, Yvonne, Suzanna, and Wesley. Then Chantelle and Emily drove to the store to collect confetti launchers and matching confetti, and thousands of balloons.

Back at the inn, Chantelle ordered the confetti launches by color, and placed them on silver platters in the living room. Each guest would be given one of each color, and when the cake was cut, revealing the gender, they were to pop the correct one. Meanwhile, Daniel got to work pumping up the balloons. It would be up to their young guests to stomp on the color they no longer needed once the reveal was made.

Once everything was done, Emily looked around at their creation. She felt a swell of excitement. This was the first time it felt really real. She'd seen her baby and soon she would discover its gender. Then she'd be able to start buying clothes and toys, decorating the nursery more. She'd be able to think about names!

They left the living room and Emily locked the door behind her. Marnie was standing in the corridor, just having descended the staircase.

"What's going on?" she asked, looking at Chantelle's sign on the door.

"Nothing," Chantelle said mischievously. "But you'll find out tonight."

"We're having a party," Emily offered. "Everyone's invited. We're just going to make the calls now. Can you let the rest of the staff know?"

Marnie looked suspicious. "Sure," she said.

Emily could tell that she was already starting to speculate about the reasons for the party. She seemed to intuitively know there was an announcement coming. Emily realized her becoming pregnant was unlikely to be a shock to anyone who knew her. It tended to follow after marriage, after all.

The family went out onto the porch, Chantelle carrying her notebook with the list of people they needed to call to invite over.

"I'll call my friends," she said, "and invite their parents too. Mommy, you call all your supplier friends like Raj and Karen. Daddy, you call everyone else."

They began making calls. But as time passed, Emily started to feel a sense of sadness. She realized that no one on their list was family. Papa Roy was uncontactable by phone. And what of their mothers? It hadn't even occurred to Chantelle to put their names on the list. The thought saddened Emily.

"What about Cassie and Patricia?" she said to Daniel.

He looked up from his cell phone where he'd been typing a number in. "I don't want my mom knowing yet," he said. "Not after the last time I saw her."

Emily thought back to the time Cassie had turned up drunk at the inn, trying to manipulate Daniel into giving her money. It had been an ugly scene. She wasn't surprised Daniel needed more time to get over it before making contact with his mother again.

But what about Patricia? The last time she'd been here, she too had caused a horrible scene. She'd been rude to Roy, rude to Emily in turn. She never seemed to be happy for Emily, or supportive. Emily didn't want anything to bring down her mood today. She would tell her mom another time.

"I'm not calling mine either," she told Daniel. "I don't want her to know yet."

He nodded in agreement.

They looked down the list of names, ticking off as they went.

"I wonder if we could get Aunt Eugenia on a video link," Daniel said. "I'd love her to be involved somehow but she obviously won't be able to fly here at such short notice."

"That's such a cool idea!" Chantelle said.

They huddled together to listen in as Daniel made the call to Aunt Eugenia and arranged a time for them to do a video call. It was so exciting knowing that she would be able to join in.

"What about Roman?" Chantelle asked, when she realized he wasn't on the list.

"I don't think he'd want to come to our little party," Emily said.

"Why not?" Chantelle challenged. "He's our friend."

"He's a megastar," Emily corrected. "He'll be busy."

"You never know if you don't ask," Chantelle said.

Emily sighed. She felt nervous calling Roman. As much as she wanted to view him as just any other person who lived in Sunset Harbor, she couldn't help but feel a little differently toward him, a little more apprehensive. His lifestyle was so lavish it made her feel plain in comparison. He'd achieved so much it made her B&B's success seem small. But he answered the call and to Emily's surprise he was utterly thrilled to be invited.

"I can hand out the confetti launchers at the door," he suggested.

With all the guests invited there was nothing else to do now but wait for the cake to be delivered.

When it arrived, it was enormous. The frosting on the outside was white but the cake in the middle would be the color of their baby's gender, and there was also a dyed gooey center that would splurge out when they cut it for maximum effect.

"That's it," Emily said once they'd said goodbye to the baker. "Everything ready."

She was excited, and felt the excitement coming from Daniel and Chantelle as well. She was just sad that there was one person missing who she really wanted to be a part of it. Her dad.

Where are you? Emily found herself wondering for what must have been the millionth time in her life. She'd really thought that her years of not knowing were over. But a leopard doesn't change its spots. Maybe her mom had been right after all, that it had been foolish of her to think she could ever trust her father again.

CHAPTER TWELVE

The moment people started to filter into the inn that night for the party, they realized what the party was for.

"Are you…?" Suzanna asked Emily, tentatively.

It was the first time Emily had seen her since baby Robin's birth. She looked gorgeous, her eyes sparkling. But Emily could also read relief in her eyes. She must be grateful to have a sitter around so she had a few hours off mommy duties!

Emily nodded excitedly. "How did you guess?" she quipped.

"With the room filled to the brim with pink and blue balloons, it was hard to miss," Suzanna replied with a laugh.

Wesley congratulated Emily with a kiss on the cheek. "I'm so thrilled for you both," he said. "Our little ones can be friends, just like our eldest ones are."

Emily grinned and nodded. She was grateful to know she'd have someone to help her through the scary beginning stages of having a newborn.

Yvonne and Keiran arrived next. Bailey, ever the firecracker, ran straight into the living room and began throwing balloons in the air. Emily wondered what she would do if she had a child with such exuberance as Bailey. She would never be able to keep up. Bailey had boundless energy!

"I can't believe it," Yvonne cried, embracing Emily tightly. "This is such fantastic news."

"Thank you," Emily replied with a little blush. "I wasn't expecting it to happen quite so soon after the wedding, but we're thrilled." She touched her stomach, thinking of the baby growing inside of her, which, according to her size chart, was now as big as a lemon.

The room began to fill up with friends. Chantelle set her laptop up in the corner and called Aunt Eugenia. Emily hovered over Chantelle's shoulder, wringing her hands with apprehension. When Aunt Eugenia answered and the screen filled with her jolly face, she immediately guessed the purpose of the call.

"I'm going to be a great-aunty?" she said.

Chantelle nodded. "And today is the gender reveal! Do you want to guess what it's going to be?"

"A boy," Eugenia said with a definitive nod. "Definitely."

"Okay," Chantelle replied. She added a tally to her notebook of who'd guessed boy and who'd guessed girl. Currently, boy was leading. "That's what most people here think too."

Emily considered the possibility of a son once more. She could picture herself more easily with a daughter, perhaps because of her experience with Chantelle. But a son would be just as wonderful. She was eager to find out.

Amy and Harry arrived next, looking as smitten as ever. George was also with them. He kissed Emily's cheek and shook hands with Daniel.

"Harry's been telling me all about the restaurant idea," he said. "I think it's great! I can't wait to find out what you guys do together." Then in a slightly quieter voice, he added, "Thanks for encouraging my little bro. He can be a bit unfocused at times. This has been his dream for ages and I'm pleased to see it might be about to finally happen."

"I think you should thank Amy, not us," Emily said. "She has a magic way of making people realize their full potential. I believe it's achieved through a combination of cajoling and stubbornness."

George laughed. "Yes, they do seem very well suited together. I haven't seen Harry like this ever!"

Emily grinned, happy to hear that Amy's impact on Harry was proving as positive as his on her.

Finally, everyone on the guest list had arrived. In one hand they all held a confetti dispenser filled with blue confetti, in the other one filled with pink. Keiran, Yvonne, Wesley, and Suzanna were in their positions in the corner of the room, holding the paper chains, ready to pin them into place.

Everyone held their breath and gasped with wonder as the enormous white frosted cake was wheeled in. Emily felt her heart fluttering with anticipation. Daniel joined her at her side, grinning sheepishly.

"Ready?" he said.

Emily nodded, though her insides swirled and whirred. Together they picked up the large knife, Daniel's hands wrapped around Emily's. The last time they'd done this had been at the wedding. It had been one of the most beautiful moments of Emily's life, and she realized that this moment too would join it. Thanks to

Daniel, to her family, she'd added more happy memories in the last few months than ever before in her life. She felt blessed as she held the knife and tried to steady her trembling hands.

"You're shaking," Daniel's voice whispered into her ear.

She felt comforted by his presence. By his solid body behind her. This moment was overwhelming her with love.

"I'm nervous," she said. "Let's do it."

She felt Daniel's nod, his head close enough to hers to touch. It was a wonderful, beautifully intimate moment. Together, they sliced into the cake. One cut. Then they moved the knife and cut the other side of the piece. They slid the knife under the base of the piece they'd cut.

Daniel counted them down. "Three. Two. One."

They pulled the slice out of the cake.

Pink.

The sponge was pink.

The gooey pink center cascaded down the sponge.

The room erupted in a surprised shout.

"A girl!" people cried.

All around Emily, pink confetti burst into the air. The sound of popping balloons from the kids stamping on the blue ones became a sudden cacophony of noise. Across the ceiling, the pink paper chains were tugged, making a criss-cross above them.

Emily hunkered down, thrilled, exhilarated, feeling happier than ever. Daniel's arms were around her, tightening in an embrace from behind. Then suddenly Chantelle catapulted through the crowd and hugged them both tightly.

"A sister! A sister!" she exclaimed.

Emily felt tears spring into her eyes. Seeing the joy that people had for her and her family meant the world to her.

This truly was one of the happiest moments of her life.

*

After much dancing, cake eating, and balloon popping, Emily's friends started to depart. It had been a delightful evening and Emily was filled with gratitude.

Once everyone was gone, Emily, Daniel, and Chantelle sat in the dining room and had dinner.

"I was thinking about baby names," Emily said.

"Me too," Chantelle replied. "I was thinking a color would be nice. Like Ruby. Or Scarlett."

"I thought it would be nice to repeat the 'elle' sound that Chantelle has," Daniel added. "Something like Isabelle. Or Gabrielle."

But that wasn't what Emily had in mind. "They're nice names," she said. "But I had a different idea."

She chewed her lip, reticent, unsure whether Daniel would be on board with her suggestion.

"Well, what is it?" Daniel said.

Emily picked at the tablecloth with her fingers, delaying the moment. Finally she spoke. "I was wondering how you felt about calling her Charlotte."

There was a pause. Emily looked up at Daniel, worried that he'd hate the idea. But his gaze on her was soft and gentle, his eyes inviting.

"It's a lovely idea," he said, nodding.

"Are you sure?" Emily said, with relief.

She didn't want to make Daniel feel like he wasn't a part of this baby, that it was just hers. But naming her after Charlotte felt like an appropriate way to honor the sister who never got a chance to grow up and have her own family. That loss sat with Emily every day, but she'd always felt Charlotte's presence in this house, had always felt her smiling down upon them. She wanted to show her love for her sister, who even in spirit form only ever wanted the best for Emily.

"I'm sure," Daniel said with kind affirmation. He reached across the table and squeezed her hand.

Emily looked at Chantelle. "What do you think? Do you like the name Charlotte?"

Chantelle nodded. "I love it. But I'll call her Lotty."

Emily smiled. "That's fine by me."

Just then, they heard a noise coming from the living room. It was a sort of electronic bleeping.

"What's that?" Emily said curiously.

"It sounds like my laptop receiving a video call," Chantelle said. "Maybe Aunt Eugenia is calling back."

Everyone stood and hurried into the living room. It was still covered in pink, bits of confetti, streamers, and copious crumbs from the cake. In the corner, Chantelle's laptop flashed with an incoming call. She sat on her knees and craned her face close to the screen. Then suddenly she screamed.

"What's wrong?" Emily asked, alarmed.

Chantelle looked back at her parents, her face beaming with excitement. "It's a video call from the UK!" she screamed.

It took a moment for Emily to realize what that meant. When it dawned on her she felt suddenly overcome with emotion.

Chantelle confirmed was she was suspecting.

"It's Papa Roy!"

CHAPTER THIRTEEN

Chantelle answered the call and Roy's face filled the screen. Emily felt her breath hitch with emotion. It had been too long since she'd seen her father, had spoken to him. She hadn't even realized how much or how deeply his absence had affected her.

He looked different. Tired. Older. His lines were more pronounced, his cheeks sunken as if he'd lost some weight since they'd last been together.

"Papa Roy!" Chantelle exclaimed. "Where have you been! We missed you!"

Roy looked embarrassed. "I'm so sorry. The post office here lost your letter. I only got it last week. Then I couldn't work out how to do this video call thing at all. I had to drive to the library in the next town over to get one of their assistants to show me how to do it!"

"So you've read the letter?" Daniel asked. "You know our news?"

Roy grinned. "I have. And congratulations. I'm thrilled for you."

Emily smiled, relieved to finally have confirmation from him that the new baby was a welcome surprise. But she had a niggling sense of worry deep inside of her. Something didn't seem right. She wasn't sure if her father just felt guilty about having been AWOL for so long or if there was something more.

"You just missed the party," Chantelle exclaimed. "We did the gender reveal!"

Roy's eyes widened slightly. "Oh? You mean you already know?"

Emily spoke next. "Yes. Do you want us to tell you?"

He nodded eagerly.

"Go on, Chantelle," Emily said, touching the child's shoulder lightly. "You tell Papa Roy."

"It's a girl!" Chantelle cried, grabbing two pink balloons in each of her hands and waving them frantically in front of the screen.

Roy seemed overcome with emotion. "That's such wonderful news. I'm so happy for you all. Baby girls are such a delight to raise."

Emily felt a lump form in her throat. "We've picked out her name already," she said. "We're calling her Charlotte."

There was a pause from Roy. He looked floored by the news. Then his eyes glittered with emotion. He wiped away a tear.

"Is that okay, Dad?" Emily asked, softly. "Do you mind?"

Roy shook his head. "Mind? Of course not. I think it's a lovely idea. I'm so happy."

Emily sighed with relief. It mattered a lot to her whether Roy was on board or not. She was so glad that this phone call had finally taken place, that he'd finally confirmed his joy at their news. It somehow made the prospect of telling her mother less terrifying. With his backing and support, she could handle whatever sniping her mom threw at her.

A crease appeared between Roy's eyebrows then as he frowned. "Emily, does that mean you can't fly now?"

"Fly?" Emily asked, confused. "I can fly up to twenty-eight weeks. Thirty-two weeks with some airlines. But why do you ask?"

"Because of the vacation," he stated. "Remember? You were all going to come and visit me for the summer."

Chantelle started bouncing on her knees. She clasped her hands together and looked up expectantly at her parents. "Are we going to England? Are we going to visit Papa Roy?"

Emily felt shell-shocked. She'd gone from having no contact with her dad to suddenly discovering he wanted them to visit, something she had finally come to term with not happening—at least not this soon.

"We can take it very easy," Papa Roy added. "Nothing too strenuous for you in your delicate state."

Emily didn't need convincing. "We'd love to come!" she cried. She looked over at Daniel for confirmation. There was a smile on his face and Emily knew that meant he agreed.

"When can you come?" Roy asked.

"We'll look at flights tonight," Emily said. "But Dad, how will we let you know when we're coming, when our flight has arrived, that sort of thing?" She couldn't help but feel worried. What if he went AWOL again? What if they flew to England and he didn't come to meet them? Anything could happen with Roy.

"I'll check in at the library every day. You can email me. And write. And then I'll call. We'll cover every base. Double, triple, quadruple check."

Chantelle laughed. She seemed so excited at the prospect of a vacation. Emily wondered whether Amy would mind them disappearing from Sunset Harbor when she herself was here all summer. But then she reminded herself that Amy was busy with Harry. She'd probably be relieved to not have to split her time between her hormonal pregnant friend and her exciting new lover!

"Okay," Emily said, reassured that this was the best thing for the family to be doing. "I'll let you know as soon as our flights are booked."

Roy smiled. "I can't wait."

Emily didn't want the call to end. She'd missed her father so much and this just didn't seem like an adequate amount of communication. It didn't make up for all the weeks she'd been worrying, for that void that had been left in her life after Roy returned to England.

"We'll see you soon, Dad," she said, trying not to let the melancholy creep into her voice.

"Soon," he said with a final smile.

Then the call cut out. Roy was gone.

Emily just hoped that the vacation would go without a hitch. She couldn't help but feel like something had changed with Roy, that there was something he wasn't telling her. She tried to calm her paranoia, remind herself it was probably just pregnancy hormones making her unnecessarily anxious. But that sense of unease stayed with her and she knew it would only be shaken once she was face to face with her father once again.

The trip to England couldn't come soon enough.

CHAPTER FOURTEEN

Daniel peered at the laptop screen, scrolling down through all the available flights.

"It's all booked up," he said. "I can't find any flights for three over the summer."

Emily felt her stomach churn with apprehension. Had they left it too late to visit Papa Roy? They could always go after the summer but she didn't want to take Chantelle out of school for it.

"Wait," Daniel said, pausing. He looked over his shoulder at Emily. "I've found some. But they're for tomorrow morning."

"Tomorrow?" Emily exclaimed, raising her eyebrows. "We can't go on such short notice!"

Chantelle tugged on her sleeve beside her. "Please, Mommy. If we don't go tomorrow we won't be able to go at all."

Emily chewed her lip. It seemed very rash to just hop on a plane and fly away on such short notice. What about the inn? She hadn't even finalized the shifts for the week. And what of the renovation work that was taking place? Daniel was supposed to be project manager, he was needed onsite overseeing everything. They couldn't just drop their responsibilities and leave.

But Emily desperately wanted to see Roy and get to the bottom of the uneasy feeling his call had stirred within her. She missed him so much and wanted to see him badly.

Then when she looked at Chantelle's sad eyes she knew there was no way she could deny the child her Papa Roy. To dash her hopes was too cruel.

"Okay," she finally said. "Let's fly out tomorrow."

Chantelle's face cracked with joy. "Really?"

Daniel spoke next. "Are you sure you're sure?"

Emily most definitely wasn't sure but she wasn't going to change her mind now. "I'll have to tidy up all the lose ends here overnight," she said. "But other than that, I'm sure. What time will we have to leave here?"

Daniel calculated back on his fingers the amount of time it would take to drive to the airport and the amount of time they'd need to get through security and check-in. "Five a.m.," he said with a wince.

Emily didn't like the sound of that. Staying up late to work, then leaving ridiculously early for the flight, was literally the opposite of what Doctor Arkwright had advised her. Minimal stress, maximum rest was the furthest thing from their plan.

At least Chantelle looked excited by the early start. "We can watch the sunrise," she grinned. "Will Matthew make us pancakes?"

"Absolutely not," Emily replied, laughing. "Matthew will be fast asleep at five a.m. like the rest of the town! We'll have to make something now so we can just grab it and go."

This just made Chantelle more excited than ever. They went down to the kitchen and cooked up some bacon for the breakfast bagels, which they covered in plastic wrap and placed in the fridge ready to grab tomorrow. In the living room, Emily could hear the Magic Elves clearing up the detritus left from the party.

She checked her watch. It was already midnight and there was so much to do before she'd feel able to leave the inn for a week.

"You need to get to bed," Emily told Chantelle. "It's way past your bedtime. Ask Daddy to tuck you in and pack the suitcases, okay? I have to sort out the schedules and send some supplier orders."

Chantelle ran off upstairs and Emily went into the study for some quiet. She worked as fast as possible but already was exhausted. Baby Charlotte may only be the size of a lemon but she was zapping all of Emily's energy and resources!

An hour passed before she'd finished all the work that needed to be done. Wearily, she trudged upstairs to see how Daniel was getting on. She found him in Chantelle's room. To her surprise, the child was sitting cross-legged on the middle of her bed, wide-eyed, cuddling a teddy.

"Someone was too excited to sleep," Daniel explained.

Emily sighed. Tired Chantelle could be a handful at times. She wasn't thrilled at the prospect of flying exhausted with an irritable child.

"It's my first ever time abroad," Chantelle said as a way of explanation. "I've never been on a plane. Actually, I've never even been on a vacation."

It made Emily's heart ache to think of all the things the child had missed out on. She was glad that as her mom she now had the opportunity to make up for missed time, to give her all the experiences she deserved. Maybe letting her stay up wasn't such a bad idea. A little treat for her.

"I'd better send an email to Jack," Daniel said. "He can take over managing the work at the spa."

"What about Trevor's?" Emily asked as she folded up one of Chantelle's summer dresses and placed it in the case. "Do you think the reno team will be okay without our supervision?"

"Of course," Daniel reassured her. "They're professionals. If Erik & Sons think they're up for the job then I trust them."

Emily couldn't help but feel nervous. Even Daniel's reassurance didn't calm her nerves.

"You guys finish packing," she said. "I'm going to go and speak to the staff."

Emily went downstairs and gathered everyone who was on the night shift together in the lounge. It was just Marnie, Lois, and Trent.

"This is a bit short notice, but we're going on a last-minute vacation," she told them. "Tomorrow."

Marnie raised an eyebrow. "That is very last minute!" she said. "Who are you putting in charge?"

"Serena is the most senior staff member," Emily said. "But she's not doing a shift this week. Neither is Parker. So..." She looked up at Lois expectantly. Once Lois had been a terrible employee. It had taken ages for her to learn the ropes. But now she was a dedicated worker and Emily trusted her to run the inn. "Lois? What do you say?"

Lois seemed to pale. "I can't be in charge," she stammered. "I'm too young. Why not Vanessa?"

Emily gave Lois a reassuring look. "Vanessa's a chambermaid. She can't be in charge. You can do this, Lois. I trust you."

Lois remained pale but she nodded.

"You guys will respect Lois while she's temporarily in charge, won't you?" Emily said, looking at the others.

They all nodded.

Emily left the meeting and went back upstairs to finish packing with Daniel and Chantelle.

"How did they take it?" Daniel asked.

"Fine. Well, sort of. Lois looks terrified about being in charge."

“I’m not surprised,” Daniel said. “She’s terrified by everything. Are you sure she’s the best person to oversee things? What about Serena?”

Emily sighed sadly. Serena was becoming more and more distant these days. She was so busy with her artwork, looking after Rico’s store, and her relationship with Owen, she hardly had the time for shifts at the inn. It saddened Emily. She didn’t want them to drift apart.

“She’s too busy.” Emily started to worry again. Maybe leaving Lois in charge was a bad plan. “I’ll speak to Amy as well. See if she’ll be able to look in once a day for me. She’d have no qualms taking the reins if need be.”

“I think that’s a good idea,” Daniel said.

Emily quickly sent a message to Amy asking her to keep an eye on the inn while she was gone and Amy replied with an emphatic yes.

With everything finalized there was only one more thing to do. Sleep! In the morning they’d be leaving for England, for Roy, and Emily couldn’t be more relieved to know she’d soon be reunited with her father.

CHAPTER FIFTEEN

Sleep-deprived and nauseous, Emily watched on as Chantelle stood against the glass windows in the airport lounge, staring at the planes with eyes like saucers. The child seemed beyond excited to take her first ever flight.

Just then, the boarding call for their flight was made.

"That's us," Daniel told Chantelle, taking her by the hand.

She skipped along beside him, Emily a little way behind them rubbing her stomach to try and calm the swirling sensation inside.

They queued to get onboard, Chantelle barely able to stand still, then finally made it onto the plane. Chantelle looked around in awe.

They took their seats.

"Why don't you sleep for a bit?" Daniel suggested to Emily. "You're looking a bit peaked."

"Thanks," Emily replied, laughing with mock affront.

But she didn't need telling twice. In a matter of moments, she'd succumbed to sleep and it was only the sensation of the plane tearing down the runway that awoke her.

Her eyes pinged open, disorientated by the sudden unnatural sensation of movement. Then her stomach flipped. She only just managed to grab a bag before she threw up. Daniel's hand was on her back instantly.

"Oh no, Mommy, are you okay?" Emily heard Chantelle say with worry.

She waved her concern away. Once her stomach was finally empty, she wiped her mouth with a tissue.

"I'll get the flight steward over," Daniel said.

"It's fine," Emily replied. She touched her stomach. "Baby Charlotte just didn't like the sensation of takeoff."

She realized that was the first time she'd called the baby by her name, the first time she'd uttered Charlotte without it being shorthand for loss and grief. Even in her uncomfortable, nauseous state the thought comforted her. The new baby was going to heal a lot of old wounds. She would give her new emotions to attach to Charlotte's memory, happy ones.

The plane continued to climb. Now it was Chantelle's turn to look a bit pale. Daniel, who was sitting between the two of them, looked harried as he checked from Emily to Chantelle.

"Are you okay?" he asked the little girl.

She nodded. "It feels strange."

He stroked her hair. "I know. But you're doing really well. You're being really brave considering this is your first ever flight."

She smiled but still looked a little panicked by the whole thing. Emily was touched to witness the tender moment between them. She couldn't wait to see Daniel express such love and care for Baby Charlotte.

At last, the plane leveled out. Daniel flicked on the call light so the steward could come and attend to Emily. A woman came over, dressed smartly in a blue suit with the archetypal coiffed hairstyle and ruby red lips of a flight attendant. She was very patient and kind, offering Emily water and more bags in case she felt sick again. Then she smiled at Chantelle.

"Are you off to visit the queen in London?" she asked.

Chantelle shook her head. "No, we're going to see my Papa Roy. He's a horologist."

The flight attendant raised a curious eyebrow. "What's that?"

"Someone who makes clocks," Chantelle said with a proud grin. "He's also a gardener. We fixed a greenhouse when he visited and grew lots of plants."

"He sounds very nice," the flight attendant said.

"Oh, he is," Chantelle said with a fervent nod.

The flight attendant left to attend to another call. Chantelle looked over at Emily.

"Will Papa Roy be as nice in England as he was in Maine?" she asked.

"I don't see why not," Emily replied with a little chuckle. "Are you worried about seeing him again?"

Chantelle gave a small shrug. "I guess. Sometimes people are nice when you first meet them but then horrible afterwards. Like Sheila's friend Mindy. We watched cartoons together the first time she came to stay and she was really funny and she made me burgers with cheese. But the next time she came she was angry and mean to Sheila and me."

Emily's heart ached at the sound of Chantelle's sad tale. It hurt her to hear how betrayed the child had been in her young life by Sheila and the unsavory company she kept.

"Papa Roy won't be mean," Emily assured her. "I promise. This is going to be the best trip ever."

Chantelle seemed satisfied with Emily's response and smiled. "I wonder what his house will be like," she said, moving on swiftly—as she was wont to do—from her dark memories.

Daniel joined in. "It will have a yard," he said. "A big one. Flowers everywhere. Trees."

"And a shed," Chantelle added. "A birdbath made of stone. A pond with frogs in it."

"The house will be made of red brick," Emily suggested. "With ivy climbing up the walls."

"And there'll be a porch," Daniel said. "A step with a welcome mat on it. A rose bush by the front door."

Chantelle giggled. "I'm going to draw a picture. Then when we get there we can compare it and see how close we got."

Daniel found some paper and coloring pens for her in their carry-on case. Chantelle got straight to work. Emily smiled to herself, knowing that she would likely be occupied for hours now, lost in her creative activity. By the look in his eye, Emily thought that Daniel was thinking the same thing.

"Why don't you sleep now?" he suggested.

Emily nodded. Keeping her eyes open was becoming impossible. She curled her arms protectively around Baby Charlotte and dozed off within a matter of moments.

*

As she slept, Emily dreamed. Unsurprisingly, it was her father who entered her unconscious mind. Now when he appeared to her in her sleep he looked as he did when he'd visited, rather than as the younger man he'd been when he walked out on her.

In her dream, Emily found herself alone in a large field. She was a child, wearing a summer dress and sandals. But the weather was gray, dark clouds racing across the sky. All at once, rain lashed around her, soaking her dress and hair. Wind ripped through the leaves of a tree that bowed ominously from the force of the wind, its branches stretching for her. Emily felt herself become panicked.

Suddenly, lightning jagged through the sky and she screamed. She ran, splashing through the muddy field, tearing in the direction of the place she knew was her home. Then Roy materialized before her, lit by another spark of lightning.

"Emily Jane!" he called to her, crouching down, stretching his arms out to her.

She rushed into them, her body colliding against his with relief, and flung her arms around his neck, holding on tightly. He heaved her up and stood. She held on tight, filled with relief as he raced them the rest of the distance to the house, rain hammering down upon them. Daddy had rescued her, again. Her hero. Like always.

Emily awoke with a start, shocked to find herself back on the airplane. The dream had felt so vivid, so real. Was it a dream or a memory? She couldn't even be sure.

She looked over and saw that Daniel was sitting in the middle seat as before, Chantelle next to him gazing out the window. Daniel turned as she stirred.

"You're awake," he said, stroking her hand tenderly. "You've been out for hours."

Emily rubbed her eyes. "I have? What time is it?"

Daniel chuckled. "We're about to start our descent."

Emily couldn't believe it. She had been asleep for hours!

"Hi, Mommy," Chantelle said then, noticing that Emily was awake. "You missed the whole flight. They showed a Disney movie, and we ate sandwiches. Daddy bought me a magazine from the nice flight attendant lady and we did the crossword, the coloring in picture, and read all the stories. Then there was turb-ee-lence…"

"Turbulence," Daniel corrected.

"Turb-u-lence," Chantelle repeated. "And I spilled my orange juice, but they gave me another one. I wasn't scared, it was like a rollercoaster. Then when it was over we played card games."

Emily raised her eyebrows. "Sounds like you've been having a lot of fun," she said, still shocked by the fact she'd slept like a log through it all. Maybe the rocky journey had infiltrated her mind slightly, causing her to dream of the rain and lightning, causing the sensation of panic she'd felt.

Daniel chuckled again and kissed Emily's forehead. "Does Baby Charlotte want anything to eat or drink?" he asked.

Emily shook her head. "I'd better not risk it. I can eat when we land."

Just then the pilot spoke over the intercom, instructing the cabin crew to take their seats for final approach.

"This is the fun part," Daniel told Chantelle. "We're going to drop down and you'll get to see all the houses and cars and animals getting bigger and bigger."

Chantelle looked excited. She turned her gaze out the window. Emily was glad for Daniel's calmness; Baby Charlotte disliked the descending sensation just as much as she'd disliked the climb. At least this time Emily was awake and able to take deep, meditative breaths to keep the nausea at bay.

She peered across the seats next to her and out the small window, watching as the plane dipped into the layer of cloud. It juddered and she instinctively clutched the armrest. Daniel's protective hand was instantly on hers, squeezing reassuringly. They broke though the cloud and the English fields and hillsides appeared beneath them. It looked absolutely beautiful.

The ground whooshed toward them and then suddenly there was a bump as the plane touched down. Emily gritted her teeth at the familiar, unpleasant rushing sensation that came from the plane decelerating so quickly, then at last they were at taxiing speed, bobbing along the runway.

"That was awesome!" Chantelle cried, looking from the window to her parents beside her.

"I'm glad someone enjoyed it," Emily replied.

Daniel stroked her tummy.

"Poor Charlotte," Chantelle said. "I hope she likes flying after she's born because I want to do it allllll the time!"

Everyone laughed.

The plane turned into its parking spot and the whirring from the engines reduced. The seatbelt sign pinged off.

"Let's go before the rush," Daniel said.

They grabbed their hand luggage from the overhead locker and hurried down the aisle. The air steward who'd been kind to Chantelle throughout the flight was waiting at the doors to bid them farewell.

"Enjoy your visit to Papa Roy," she said with a smile.

"Thanks! I will!" Chantelle cried, eager to get off the plane and onto English soil.

They left the plane, breathing fresh air for the first time in hours, and headed into the arrivals terminal to collect their bags.

"Where will Papa Roy be?" Chantelle asked impatiently.

Emily checked her phone. As promised, he'd sent her both an email and a text message confirming he would be meeting them on landing.

"He'll be meeting us after we've collected our bags," Emily told her.

Chantelle stared at the carousel of luggage as it passed in front of them. Her expression was one of utter impatience. Emily couldn't help but laugh to herself at the child's expressiveness.

Finally they saw their luggage. They heaved their bags off the conveyor belt and Chantelle led the way, hurrying through the corridors with the kind of haste people would expect from someone who was late for their flight, not someone who'd just arrived.

They burst out into the arrivals lounge and searched the crowd of people for Papa Roy.

"There he is!" Chantelle cried.

She abandoned her bags and went running past people, heading for her beloved grandfather. Daniel scooped her discarded bag up with a chuckle. Emily watched on, smiling, as Chantelle reached Roy and leapt into his outstretched arms. It was a beautiful reunion to behold.

The two were still hugging tightly when Daniel and Emily reached them. As Roy set Chantelle back down on her feet, Emily noticed that he was indeed thinner than he had been at the wedding. She couldn't help but instantly worry. The nagging concerns she'd felt earlier were only amplified by seeing him in the flesh.

"Dad," she said, wrapping her arms around his neck.

He held her tightly, his body more wiry than it had been before. He'd lost his layer of squish.

"My darling," he whispered into her ear with deep feeling. "I've missed you so much."

"I've missed you too," Emily replied, feeling herself choke up.

They released one another and next it was Daniel's turn to embrace Roy. Emily found their reunion just as touching to witness as Chantelle's had been.

"My deepest congratulations to you both," Roy said once he and Daniel finished embracing. He looked at Emily's stomach. "May I?"

"Of course," Emily said. "There's nothing to feel yet, though. Baby Charlotte is only the size of a lemon at the moment."

Roy touched her stomach gently. "No kicks?"

Emily shook her head. "Just flutters at the moment. Soon though." She smiled.

Roy removed his hand. "Right, we'd best get in the car. It's still a bit of a drive from here, but I'll take us the scenic route so we can take in the glorious English countryside route rather than the not so glorious English motorway route."

They left the airport, laden with bags, and headed for Papa Roy's car.

The drive to Roy's house took an hour or so. Chantelle spent the whole time narrating the journey. She pointed out every cow, every quaint cottage, and read aloud all the town names from the signposts using her best British accent. Emily found it thoroughly amusing.

"Look, it's the ocean!" Chantelle cried.

Everyone turned to look out across the beautiful seaside, with houses and stores built right up to the beach. It was gorgeous. Emily could see why her father liked this place so much. It reminded her of Sunset Harbor in many ways.

When they pulled up outside Roy's house, Emily realized just how much of their predictions were correct. It was a stone cottage with a porch, rose bushes, and creeping ivy climbing the walls. The lawn was large and lush, sloping downhill and stretching on forever. Wild flowers bloomed everywhere, a patchwork of vibrant color. To the left, framing the house, were hillsides dotted with horses. The rolling hills seemed to encase the house which was nestled snug within a valley. To the right was something they had not predicted; a cliffside overlooking the harbor, and beautiful views over the crashing ocean.

It was like a paradise here.

"This is amazing," Chantelle announced breathlessly. She looked as though she'd stepped into a dream, or perhaps into the pages of a fantasy novel.

"Let me show you inside," Roy said.

He led the way and they followed. Inside, the cottage had rather low ceilings with wooden beams. Daniel had to bow his head so as not to bump it.

"It's very cozy," Emily commented, looking at the shelf-lined walls crammed with books, the window seat to read them in.

"It smells like old things," Chantelle commented.

Papa Roy laughed. "That's because it's filled with antiques," he said. "And clocks."

He led them through the small living room, which had little more than a comfortable beige fabric couch, a fireplace, and a deep red, threadbare Persian rug inside of it, then into a hallway.

"It's a bit of a maze here," he said. "I like to joke that it's like a rabbit warren."

It seemed very fitting for him, Emily thought. Roy could never be content living in a place that wasn't illogical, filled with strange rooms, winding corridors, and wonky ceilings.

Emily heard the sound of syncopated ticking coming from behind a door.

"What's in here, Dad?" she asked.

"Ah," Roy said with a grin. He turned the doorknob and pushed it open, revealing a room that smelled of dust and metal, and was filled to the brim with clocks. "My workroom."

Emily gasped as she stepped inside. This room was by far the biggest in the whole house, and of course her father had decided to use it for his beloved clocks rather than as a recreation space. She looked about her at all the half-finished clocks. Some were enormous. There were even several grandfather clocks propped up against one wall.

"Chantelle, you'll like this one," Roy said, beckoning the child over.

She approached him eagerly. Roy flicked a switch at the side of a six-foot-tall grandfather clock and the door swung open. A panel folded down and clicked into place. Emily realized with delighted surprise that it doubled up as a small stool, with a padded cushion on top. Behind the panel it had been concealing a small shelf with several books. Everyone clapped with delight.

"It's a secret reading room," Roy explained. "I was commissioned to make it by a lady for her daughter."

"It's fabulous," Emily exclaimed.

Chantelle laughed with pleasure. "What else, Papa Roy? What other things have you made?"

"Let me show you."

Roy led them into the kitchen, which was very rustic. It was quite messy but in a nice, lived-in way. On the work surface there were more clock pieces, and the dining table was covered in jewelry.

"I thought you said that was your workroom," Daniel joked.

Roy grinned. "Honestly, everywhere is my workroom." He laughed and picked something up from the table. It looked like a locket. He handed it to Chantelle. "This isn't quite finished yet. But look, if you twist this here…"

He handed it to her. She twisted the dial and the front layer popped open revealing an intricately carved metal tree inside. It reminded Emily of the amazing locket he'd made her for her wedding.

Chantelle squealed. "It's amazing!" she cried.

"It will be even better when I've added the sparkles," he said. He snapped it shut with relish, reminding Emily of a magician, then put the locket back out of sight. "Now who wants a nice cup of tea?"

Everyone nodded and Roy bustled over to the kettle. He made up a pot of tea in a white ceramic, chipped pot, then set it down on the table.

"Hey, look," Chantelle said, pointing at the oven in the distance. "It's a picture of me!"

Emily squinted through the steam as Roy poured the tea. There were several photographs hanging beside the Aga oven. Some were Chantelle, some Daniel, even Mogsy and Rain were in one of the pictures. But the vast majority were of Emily and Charlotte in their youths.

Emily stood and paced over, her breath catching at the sight of the unfamiliar photographs. She'd thought her father had left all of them behind when he'd run off. Yet here was proof that he'd never stopped thinking of her or Charlotte. The pictures were faded, but showed them in various places; the garden, the beach, next to a snowman. Emily felt tears well in her eyes.

She returned to the table and sipped her tea quietly, thinking over the pictures, lost in thoughts and memories. She was jolted back to the moment by everyone standing, their cups now drained.

"Papa Roy's showing us our rooms," Chantelle explained.

"Oh, of course," Emily said, coming back to the moment.

Roy led them up the rickety staircase. "There's enough room for you to have a separate room, Chantelle. So I've put a bed in here for you."

He opened up a door and Chantelle peered in. The room was very small, but very cozy. Roy had made up a bed that was halfway between a nest and a den, with pillows everywhere and fabric hanging from the ceiling. Chantelle gasped in wonder.

"I love it!" she gushed, dumping her bag down.

In the next room, there was a double bed for Emily and Daniel.

"This is my room usually," Roy explained. "But I'm going to sleep in the guest room as it's only got a single bed. Plus this one is closer to the bathroom, which will be useful for morning sickness."

"Are you sure?" Emily asked. "I don't want to put you out."

"I'm certain," Roy said.

They went inside. Emily noticed there were many, many more photographs in here, as well, of her and Charlotte and some of the beautiful places in Sunset Harbor. There were also pictures from Roy's home in Greece, and one of him with a group of other elderly people looking very tanned next to a fig tree. She smiled, happy to know her father had company.

"Now you've had the tour and dropped your bags off," Roy said. "Who wants to go and see the town?"

Chantelle jumped up and down with excitement. "Me!" she cried.

Daniel looked at Emily. "What do you think? Are you too tired?"

Emily laughed. "I just slept for the entire flight. I have plenty of energy to see the town. Let's go!"

CHAPTER SIXTEEN

They decided against taking the car, instead taking in the sights of Falmouth by foot.

"This is the River Fal," Roy explained, his arm looped through Chantelle's.

"It's so pretty here," Chantelle replied.

The streets were narrow, cobbled in places and lined on both sides by three-story white townhouses. Bright bunting criss-crossed the high street, which was peppered by market stalls.

Emily's attention was drawn to a glass-fronted store, displaying several artworks in its windows. Each painting depicted the beauty of Cornwall, of its harbors and cliffsides, of its rolling green fields and sparkling brooks.

"These are wonderful," Emily exclaimed. She read the signage in the window aloud. "Stocking art from internationally acclaimed Falmouth-inspired artists, from Charles Napier Hemy, Dorothea Tanning, and Henry Moore to today's Tacita Dean and David Nash." She turned to her father. "I can see why you chose to settle here. That's an impressive roll call!"

Roy chuckled. "Oh yes. Even Turner was a regular visitor to Falmouth. The town has a very rich artistic heritage." Then he added, "Now, we'd better head down to the docks. Daniel needs his fix."

Everyone laughed as they ambled along happily, heading in the direction of the water.

"A pier!" Chantelle exclaimed enthusiastically.

"This is the Prince of Wales Pier," Roy explained. "And just over there we have the new quay and the National Maritime Museum."

"There's so much to do here," Daniel enthused.

"Indeed," Roy confirmed. "We also have many festivals, my favorite being the Falmouth Oyster Festival."

"Like father, like daughter," Daniel quipped. "Emily loves her seafood!"

Emily rubbed her stomach. "I miss it so much. I can't stomach it at the moment, not while Baby Charlotte's on board."

"Not to worry," Roy said. "There are plenty of other restaurants and cafes we can eat at. What do you feel like having for lunch?"

Chantelle had already spotted somewhere, and she pointed ahead. Emily looked to where she was indicating and saw a small black van with a picture of a pig on the side.

"You want sausages for lunch?" Emily said with a laugh.

Chantelle nodded enthusiastically. They went over to the van and ordered everyone some food. To Emily's surprise it was actually very good quality. She'd been expecting a greasy hotdog but what she received was in fact a delicious, thick sausage in two slices of sourdough bread. It was delicious. Both she and Baby Charlotte were very satisfied.

"I love being in a new country," Chantelle gushed.

Emily smiled at her daughter. She seemed enamored by the place, by the brand new experience of being abroad, and Emily was grateful to have been able to give her some happy memories to treasure. Emily herself felt like she was in a dream. She was so happy to be with her father again, this time experiencing his world, his life, the place he had kept her from for over twenty years. Every time she glanced up and caught sight of him it almost struck her with surprise. She was so relieved to be back with him. But at the same time she was still worried about the change in his appearance.

He noticed her looking and came over to her. He wrapped an arm around her shoulder and gave her a sideways hug as they strolled slowly on. Emily leaned into him, comforted and content.

"How are you finding the pregnancy?" Roy asked.

"Tiring," Emily replied. "But exciting." She smiled. "Seeing her on the ultrasound scan was incredible. I have the picture in my bag at home."

"You'll have to show me once we're back."

They fell into an easy silence. Emily breathed in the fresh, warm sea air. The sound of boats gently bobbing in the harbor relaxed her even further.

"I wish you could have been there for the gender reveal party," Emily murmured. She felt so at ease in this beautiful, relaxing town, she didn't feel in the least bit concerned about bringing up her disappointment with her father. Then she added, "You should have been amongst the first people to know."

"I'm sorry," Roy replied. There was sadness in his inflection. "I didn't mean to fall off the radar again. I let life get in the way."

"It's okay," Emily said with an exhalation. Even though she shouldn't be, she was used to it. "So how is life? The clock business seems to be booming."

"It's steady," Roy replied. "I've been trying to get a little more done than usual. Increase my schedule. I want to treat you all. Now there's a baby coming as well, I'll need to work even harder."

"Dad, I don't want you to do that," Emily said. "We can care for ourselves. Daniel is already working overtime for the baby. And you're getting old now, you need to slow down. You look like you're wearing yourself into the ground."

There was a sad twinkle behind Roy's eyes. But he shook his head. "I have lots of time to make up for. I want to make sure you're comfortable for the rest of your life. I want to make sure I leave you as much as possible."

Emily was shocked to hear her father speak this way. He seemed so sad, and it was such a dark turn to the conversation.

"You've given me the inn, Dad," she reassured him. "It's become my life! What more could you possibly give me that you haven't already? Honestly, I'm deeply grateful for that house and what it's brought to my life. All I need from you is your availability, not your riches. Just write to me more. Call me more. That's how you can support me."

Roy nodded quietly. Emily squeezed his hand. He seemed to brighten again.

"So the inn is doing remarkably well, I hear," he said.

"We're rushed off our feet at the moment," Emily said. "Redesigning Trevor's, building the spa. Then we're expanding with a restaurant. It should all be ready by Labor Day. You'll have to come and see the work when it's done."

"That would be lovely," Roy said.

Emily couldn't help but hear the melancholy tone in his voice. Was he lying? She knew she could be prone to feelings of paranoia, but it sounded to Emily as if he had no intention of visiting the inn again. She wondered even more what was going on with him, her mind racing with fears.

Just then Chantelle ran over. She grabbed Emily's hand and began tugging. "There's a candy store and it sells taffy!" she cried. "Can we get some, Mommy? Please please please?"

Emily laughed, happy to have a distraction from her worries. "Of course," she said. "Let's go."

They went together into the quaint candy store, where the walls were lined with glass jars filled with colorful candy. Chantelle bought some, delighting in spending her first ten-pound note, and as equally enamored by the paper pink-and-white-striped bag they came in. Like the caring child she was, she shared them out between Daniel, Emily, Roy, and herself.

"Not too many," Emily warned. "We don't want to spoil our dinner."

"That's a good point," Roy said, his voice obscured by the hard candy he was sucking on. "I have a wonderful meal planned for you all. A roast dinner."

Chantelle looked excited. She licked her lips hungrily.

"I think we should take that as a sign," Daniel laughed. "Time to head home."

Everyone agreed and they headed back to Roy's cottage on the cliffside.

*

Emily forked the last bit of lamb and roast potato into her mouth. "Dad," she said, "that was a triumph."

"I'm glad you liked it," Roy chuckled. "Daniel? Chantelle? What did you both think?"

"The Yorkshire pudding was amazing," Daniel said. "I wish we had these back in America."

"They're very easy to make," Roy said. "I'll give you the recipe."

"I liked all of it," Chantelle said.

Emily saw that her plate was completely clean. There wasn't even any gravy left!

"I can see that," Roy said with a jovial chuckle.

Daniel and Chantelle collected the plates and took them to the kitchen to wash up together, while Emily and Roy retired to the living room.

The small room was very cozy, and Emily sunk into the large couch beside her father.

"Have you had a nice day, darling?" Roy asked.

"It's been lovely," Emily replied. She stifled a yawn. "I'm quite tired now though. That was quite a lot of walking to do after such a long flight, even if I was asleep the whole time."

Chantelle and Daniel came into the room then, having finished tidying. Daniel was carrying a tray with a teapot and mugs on it.

"I thought we might all want some after-dinner tea," he said.

"And some mint thins," Chantelle added, producing a dark green box and placing it on the tray.

"What a lovely idea," Emily agreed.

As Daniel placed the tray on the coffee table before them, Emily noticed a stack of what looked like photo albums on its middle shelf, hidden under some piles of gardening magazines. The design on their jackets looked exactly the same as the ones Daniel had salvaged from the shed during the storm when she'd first arrived at Sunset Harbor.

"Dad, can I look at these?" Emily asked, curious to see what they contained.

Roy looked confused. "Oh, I'd completely forgotten they were there. I don't even know what's in them!"

Emily picked the first one up, wiping off the layer of dust that had built up on it over the years. Chantelle came and sat beside her—dark chocolate already smeared around her mouth—eager to join in.

Emily opened up the album in her hands and was immediately floored by what she saw.

"It's me!" she exclaimed.

There were four photos on the double-page spread, each one of her as a newborn baby, in the hospital, lying in her mother's arms for the first time. Patricia looked enamored with the precious baby in her arms. Emily had never in her life seen her mother look that way, not the least at her. It was an expression of deep love. The sight brought tears to Emily's eyes.

"You were a cute baby," Daniel gushed, peering over from the other side of Roy.

"She was," Roy added. "Such beautiful big eyes. Your mother and I adored you from the second we set eyes on you."

Emily could see as much. She just wondered how it had all gone so spectacularly wrong.

She turned the page, filled with a mixture of anticipation and dread.

The next four pictures were of her again, this time surrounded by extended family members and friends. Someone had knitted her a pink hat which was placed on her head.

"Aw, Mommy!" Chantelle exclaimed. "Look at your hat!"

Everyone else was chuckling but Emily felt odd looking at the pictures, looking at these moments of her life that she couldn't remember. There had been a time when her mom and dad were happy together, happy with her, united as a family. It was an alien concept to her.

"This was when we first brought you home," Roy said.

Emily nodded silently and turned the page. Four more pictures. Four more versions of herself.

"How many photos did you take?" Emily asked, her voice a raspy whisper.

"I got a little carried away," Roy admitted. "I think I took at least one picture of you every day."

Emily's eyes widened and held up the photo album. "You mean this whole thing is filled with me?"

Roy nodded. Then he gestured to the others stacked on the coffee table shelf. "They all are."

Emily began to turn the pages a little more quickly, glancing at each picture, seeing herself grow minutely on a day-by-day basis. It was extraordinary. She'd had no idea her father had produced such detailed records of her growing up. It made sense that he would considering his character, but it was still miraculous to her.

Emily became overwhelmed then, by emotion, by loss. She felt Roy's abandonment of her again, so keenly. But she also felt more than that. She felt his own emotional turmoil. Things must have gotten so bad for him and his own mental state to make him walk away from her, when he so clearly adored her.

"Emily Jane?" Roy said gently beside her.

"I'm sorry!" Emily blurted. "I just… there's just so much here. I didn't know you'd documented all of this."

Chantelle wrapped her arms around Emily's neck. "It's okay, Mommy. We don't mind if you cry."

Emily felt comforted by her family. She felt Daniel reach over from the other side of the couch to squeeze her shoulder. Their support made her tears fall more freely.

"How many albums do you think you have?" Emily asked her dad.

He shook his head. "It's so hard to say. I sent a lot of pictures to extended family members and friends as well. I imagine there'll be quite a few scattered over the house, in the garage and attic. Then it's highly likely there's some in Maine, still others in

Greece." He looked guilty. "I'm not always the most organized person."

"I'd love to see some of Charlotte," Emily said. "If you can find them."

"Maybe another day," Daniel suggested. "I think we're all a bit tired now."

Emily nodded her agreement. She managed to dam her tears. Then they all climbed the rickety staircase, saying goodnight once they reached the landing at the top.

Inside her room, Emily sunk down into bed. She felt spent, both physically and emotionally, and wondered what else the vacation would have in store for her.

CHAPTER SEVENTEEN

Emily woke the next morning in the unfamiliar surroundings of her father's cottage. The wallpaper was fading, stripes of pink roses running down the walls. The pillow felt strange beneath her head; duck feather, she guessed.

Daniel stirred beside her. "You're awake," he said. "And not throwing up."

"You're right," Emily replied. She touched her stomach protectively. "I slept the whole night through."

"Baby Charlotte must be a fan of Roy's roast dinner," Daniel joked.

Emily watched as he slung back the covers and clambered out of the old bed, which squeaked beneath him as he stood. The extra work he'd been putting in on the spa had honed his physique even more, she noted dreamily.

"I wonder what my father has planned for us today," Emily said.

She too got out of bed, and dressed herself for the day in a loose-fitting shirt and summery skirt. She noticed that the waistband was getting tighter. Looking in the mirror that stood in the corner of the room, she noticed the changes that had begun to take place in her body. She looked rounder, a little softer and squishier, and couldn't help but muse on the fact that while Daniel seemed to be becoming buffer day by day she was becoming rounder. Meanwhile, Chantelle was growing like a beanpole and her father was shrinking. Time and circumstances were changing them all before her very eyes.

Once they were both dressed and ready for the day, Emily and Daniel went to awaken Chantelle. But they found her bed empty.

"She must be up having breakfast with Papa Roy," Emily said, remembering the way the two had enjoyed breakfasts together when he'd been staying at the inn.

They went down the narrow staircase and followed the higgledy-piggledy corridor through the lounge and out into the kitchen. Sure enough, Chantelle and Roy were both there, sitting at the large oak table still strewn with clock pieces and cogs.

"Good morning," Roy said, looking up and beaming at them.

Chantelle glanced up from the clock pieces in front of her. She was holding a screwdriver in one hand and had a magnifying eyeglass on one eye. She grinned widely.

"What's going on here?" Emily asked, amused.

"Papa Roy's teaching me how to fix clocks," Chantelle said, scratching beneath the strap that fastened the peculiar-looking eye glass in place.

"Is he now?" Emily laughed. "And how is she getting on?"

"A natural of course," Roy said.

In front of Chantelle there was also an empty bowl of oatmeal.

"You've had something for breakfast?" Emily asked.

"Papa Roy made me *porridge*," Chantelle announced. "Do you want some too?"

"I think I'll have eggs this morning," Daniel said. "Emily?"

"Just plain toast for me," Emily said, taking a seat. She felt very heavy today, like her muscles had less power in them than usual.

"Oh no, Mommy, were you sick again?" Chantelle asked with concern, putting her screwdriver down.

Emily shook her head. "No, actually. Today was the first day I didn't have morning sickness."

"It's the water," Roy said. "Soft and filled with minerals like magnesium. That's very good for settling a stomach."

"I should probably bottle some and take it home, in that case," Emily said with a laugh. "Although we might have some trouble getting it through customs."

Daniel returned to the table with his fried egg on toast and Emily's plain toast. He set it down in front of her.

"That doesn't look too appetizing, my dear," Roy said. "Why not add some of my homemade jam? It's blackberry. I forage them from the brambles myself." Then his eyes glittered with excitement. "In fact, Chantelle, we need to go berry picking while you're here! It's great fun. We can make a crumble with our winnings."

Chantelle grinned and nodded her head eagerly.

Emily smeared some of the jam on her toast but the taste was still too strong for her. "It's lovely, Dad, but I think I'll pass," she said.

As she continued with her plain breakfast, she noticed that her father wasn't actually eating anything. He just had a steaming cup of tea and a glass of juice in front of him.

"Didn't you eat anything this morning?" she asked him, a little concerned. If he was skipping breakfast that might explain the weight loss.

"I ate before you were all up," Roy explained. "I get up at daybreak so that I can water the plants and vegetable garden."

Chantelle giggled. "You're so silly, Papa Roy. The plants don't care."

"*Au contraire!*" Roy replied. "Plants prefer to be watered while it's still cool. Otherwise the water might evaporate before they've had a chance to drink their fill. Honestly, my dear, and you call yourself a gardener!"

Everyone laughed.

Just then, Daniel's phone made a noise. He checked it, frowning.

"Is everything okay?" Emily asked.

"It's Jack," Daniel replied. "He said he's pulled his back and is taking a week off work."

"Oh no," Emily said. "I hope he's okay." Then she thought of the inn. "Will it delay the renovations?"

Daniel shook his head. "No, Jack's hired a contractor to cover him. He hopes that's okay with you."

"Of course it is," Emily said, appreciating his diligence. "Wish him a speedy recovery from all of us."

Daniel quickly typed a message into his phone, then stowed it back in his pocket. "So, what's the plan for today?" he asked, finishing off the last of his breakfast.

"I thought it would be nice to take the boat out," Roy replied. "The weather is supposed to be nice today, and I know you'll be hankering to sail."

Emily didn't much like the idea of going out on the boat; she felt as if she'd cheated her morning sickness somehow and wondered whether it would retaliate by striking at a later, more embarrassing moment.

"Can we fish as well?" Chantelle asked, looking thrilled by the prospect of sailing.

"Of course," Roy said. "We can catch our supper. Herring. Mackerel. Plaice. Pollock. Cod. They all swim in our oceans and every one tastes delicious battered with a side of mushy peas and chips."

Chantelle laughed again. She looked so delighted by the outing that Emily didn't have the heart to interject. If fate was going to make her throw up on the boat trip then she was just going to have to accept it.

*

It was midday by the time they made it down to the docks, and the sun was bright in the sky.

"I didn't know England could be this sunny," Chantelle said. "I thought it was supposed to always rain."

"Not always," Roy replied. "Just almost always."

He led them to his boat. Daniel seemed very impressed.

"It's a beautiful vessel, Roy," he gushed. "It's a shame you only get a few days a year to take her out."

"I know, but it makes it all the more special when I do," Roy replied.

He got on board and helped Emily and Chantelle on in turn. Daniel followed after.

As he turned to get the motor going, Roy began to cough rather loudly.

"Dad, are you okay?" Emily asked, concerned. After his weight loss and the spiel he'd given this morning about having breakfast before any of them had woken up, her worry over him had only increased. She was oversensitive to every little sign that things might not be so great for him at the moment.

"Just a tickle at the back of my throat," Roy said, and true to his word, the coughing soon subsided.

He got the engine running and then pulled them out of the dock, heading for the ocean. Chantelle gazed out at the ocean with wonder, clutching her fishing rod ready to spring into action.

Thankfully for Emily, the water was calm today and her flavorless breakfast stayed put in her stomach. The ocean smelled very salty, though, so it wasn't entirely plain sailing for her.

As Chantelle, Roy, and Daniel began fishing, Emily lay back on the bench and caught some rays. She felt very relaxed, listening to the happy chatter of her family, feeling the gentle summer rays on her skin. In fact, it was the most relaxed she'd felt in weeks, in months even. If this was what Doctor Arkwright meant when she said to take it easy, Emily had thus far followed her advice rather woefully. She made a promise to herself to be kinder on her body when she got back home. Depending on how well Lois had handled the inn in her absence, perhaps she should consider extending her temporary leadership position, allowing Emily herself to go down to part time.

Just then, she heard cheering and exclamations. She sat up, her sun hat flopping down beside her.

"Chantelle caught a bass!" Daniel exclaimed, holding up the slippery fish. Its fins glittered in the light.

"Amazing work," Emily gushed. She was very proud of Chantelle. Not many seven-year-olds had the patience to fish, but she was becoming something of a pro.

"Well, that can be our lunch then," Roy said with a smile.

But once again he was overcome by a fit of coughing. This time, it was more than just Emily's expression that turned to concern. Chantelle looked up at her Papa Roy with fearful eyes.

"Are you sick, Papa Roy?" she asked, sounding younger than normal with her anxiety.

He waved his hands, coughing too hard to speak. Daniel handed him a bottle of water, which he sipped. Emily worried her hands in her lap as she watched on. Roy had gone quite red in the face.

Finally, he stopped coughing. "I'm fine, honestly. It's nothing."

He sounded reassuring, but Emily couldn't help the nagging worry that seemed to be growing in the back of her mind.

*

After returning to the cottage for a lunch of fish and chips, Emily started to feel very tired.

"Who would like to go for a stroll in the forest?" Roy asked, looking across the empty plates on the table at his family.

"I do!" Chantelle cried.

Emily shook her head. "I'm sorry, but I think I'm going to need to sit this one out. I'm feeling tired. I might go and take a nap, then hopefully I'll feel better for whatever is planned for the evening."

Daniel looked worried. He rubbed her shoulders tenderly. "I'll stay here with you. Roy, Chantelle, do you mind taking a stroll on your own?"

"Not at all," Roy said. "You know I relish any opportunity to chat with my sweet granddaughter."

He ruffled her hair. Chantelle grinned from ear to ear.

"Are there brambles in the forest?" she asked.

Roy snapped his fingers as if she'd had a triumphant idea. "Of course there are! Let's take a basket and fill it with blackberries. Then if your mom is still snoozing when we get back we can make her a crumble."

"That sounds like a lovely way to be woken up," Emily agreed.

Chantelle and Roy put on their jackets and collected a wicker basket for the berries, which Chantelle carried over her arm. It reminded Emily of when she'd been a flower girl at the wedding, distributing petals from her basket onto the aisle, and she smiled to herself at the memory.

She and Daniel saw the two of them out, waving as they strolled light-footedly down the path, across the garden, and out the gate. Then Daniel scooped his arm around her waist and led her back inside.

They retired to the living room. Emily tucked her feet up under her as she snuggled into the comfortable, old couch.

"Is Baby Charlotte causing a fuss?" Daniel asked as he sat beside Emily and pressed his hand against her stomach.

"It's not her so much," Emily confessed, "although it's not exactly a picnic in the park growing a human being inside of you!" Daniel laughed and Emily continued. "I think it's the emotion of being here that is tiring me out. All those photographs I've never seen before. Being in my father's world after having no contact with him for so long. I mean, this is what he was doing for all those years! Fixing clocks and making jam and buying art from stores with pretty bunting outside. All the while I had no idea whether he was even alive or not. I just can't quite gather my thoughts properly."

Daniel wrapped her in his arms and held her tightly. "I know. It must be very difficult for you."

Emily sighed, sinking against his chest, feeling comforted by his solidness. "I wonder what life would have been like if I had known. If he'd just gone about it all better. If he'd just told me that he was leaving, moving abroad. Can you imagine if I'd spent my summers here as a teenager, rather than with my mom in New York City? Or if I'd moved here? I might well have done so if the opportunity was there, to get away from her."

She felt Daniel's arms tighten around her. "I know it doesn't always feel like it," he said in a reassuring tone. "But things do happen for a reason. If you'd moved to England with your dad, then we would never have met." He touched her stomach. "Baby Charlotte wouldn't exist."

"You're right," Emily said. "Things happened the way they did for a reason. The journey was difficult but I wouldn't change it, not if it meant losing you or Chantelle or Baby Charlotte. It's just so hard not to think about what could have been."

Daniel pressed a kiss against the crown of her head and they held each other, Emily finding comfort in the sound of his heartbeat. Despite the difficult things she'd been through, if they had been necessary to lead her to this time and this place, to make her this person with this life, then it was all worth it.

CHAPTER EIGHTEEN

The vacation seemed to sift away from them as quickly as sand. From Roy and Chantelle's home-cooked Cornish pasties and Victoria sponge cakes, to their garden tending, flowering arranging, and clock fixing, Emily felt that a week just wasn't long enough for the family to catch up properly with her father. Chantelle demanded vast amounts of time with him and Emily felt like she didn't get as much of an opportunity to speak to him, though that was equally from pregnancy symptoms. She felt like she'd hardly had a chance to take in the beauty of the local area, so when Roy told them they were going on a very special outing, Emily had been determined not to be left behind.

Despite her sickness, she clambered into Roy's car with the others. He drove them up the hillsides to a place called Trebah Gardens. He parked in the lot at the top and everyone got out of the car.

They walked together toward the edge of the hill and the view opened up before them. Wind rustled through Emily's hair as she gazed down across the treetops and down, down, down into a valley of dark green vegetation. It was so beautiful she could hardly catch her breath.

The garden was built on a hillside that led all the way down to the river, beach, and ocean at the bottom. From here, Emily's entire field of vision was filled with the spectacular view.

"Dad, this place is absolutely stunning," she gasped, looking across at Roy.

She thought she noticed a hint of melancholy in his expression as he, too, gazed down at the scene before them.

"It's one of the most beautiful places in Cornwall," he said, somewhat wistfully. "My favorite."

"Mine too," Chantelle agreed.

"But you've hardly seen any of it," Roy said with a laugh.

Emily noticed the way he seemed to snap out of whatever thoughts he'd gotten lost in whenever it came to speaking to Chantelle. She recognized the trait in him as one he'd used with her as a child. It was his attempt to conceal bad news or downplay bad vibes. She could still vividly remember him behaving that way after one of her parents' many screaming matches. He would just suddenly change, his whole demeanor shifting. It comforted her when she was a child, but now she could see through it. Roy was putting on a brave face, an act. There was something he wasn't telling her.

She watched as he held his hand out to Chantelle, his grin wide and inviting, and added, "It gets better and better and better as you go. Are you ready?"

They began to amble slowly down the hillside. The gardens were stunning, filled with unusual tropical plants, tree ferns, and towering bamboo.

"What is this?" Chantelle asked, staring up in amazement at a strange plant that looked like a spinach shrub for a giant.

"I believe that's gunnera," Roy told her. "Also known as giant rhubarb."

"We could make the biggest crumble in the world out of that," Chantelle uttered.

"It's usually native to Latin America so goodness knows what they've done to make it grow here!"

They continued on down the valley, passing statues and art installations hidden in the trees. The garden was filled with hydrangeas of every conceivable color, from white to pink to violet, making the place burst with summer color. Chantelle found a tiny thatch-roofed house hidden amongst the shrubbery, and a play area for children tucked away behind the trees.

As Chantelle burned off some of her energy on the swings and climbing frame, Emily took a moment to revel in the peace and natural beauty surrounding her. Then she heard a sound.

"What was that?" she asked Daniel who was close by.

"It sounded like quacking to me," he replied.

Emily wandered over to where the sound had come through. Peeking through the trees she found several ponds full of mallards. She laughed with delight, watching them preen their feathers and dive under the water.

Across the pond was a cute, rickety-looking wooden bridge.

"It looks just like the Monet painting of the bridge over the lily pond," Emily gushed.

Feeling like a child, she hurried across the bridge, swinging her arms wide, enjoying the carefree moment. Dappled sunshine warmed her skin.

The rest of the family followed, catching up with her on the other side, and they continued on together. They took the route alongside a stream, the water providing a babbling backdrop as they wandered. The trees here were mature ones—oaks and maples.

Emily felt like she was suddenly in a forest.

Then all at once, they had reached the bottom of the valley. The trees thinned to reveal the bay—tranquil and private—and the glittering ocean. They took it in turns to take the narrow bridge across the river—the final hurdle between them and the beach—then hurried out onto the sand.

"Now I see why you told us to bring our swimming things," Chantelle said to Roy.

"And a picnic," Emily added. "I don't know about you all, but I'm starving."

They spread a blanket out on the sand and took out the sandwiches and snacks they'd prepared in Roy's kitchen that morning. While Emily ate, Chantelle changed into her swimsuit and charged off into the water as soon as she'd swallowed her last mouthful.

"There's a stall over there where you can buy coffee," Roy said.

Daniel immediately perked up and hurried off to purchase his caffeine fix. When he returned a moment later his arms were laden with ice creams.

"I got a bit carried away," he said.

From the ocean, Chantelle must have spotted Daniel because she suddenly hurried back and pelted across the beach toward them.

"Ice cream!" she cried, flinging herself down onto the blanket.

Daniel passed them around and Emily took the pistachio-and-rose-flavored one. It tasted divine.

"Baby Charlotte approves," she said.

They spent several hours relaxing on the beach, eating, swimming, and chatting about life. Emily was so grateful that they'd come to Trebah Gardens. It had been the highlight of her entire trip; a wholesome, rejuvenating experience.

The air was starting to cool a little.

"Maybe we should start heading back up," Daniel suggested. "It will take us longer to get up than it did down and the light is going to start fading soon."

Though Emily agreed, she felt a tinge of sadness over the fact this moment couldn't go on forever. And if this moment couldn't, then neither could the next, nor the one after that. Before they new it, the holiday would be over. They would have to leave, back on a plane to Maine. Emily didn't feel ready for that to happen.

They packed up the picnic and wrapped Chantelle up in a towel, then ambled slowly back up through the gardens. The sky began to dim, offering them a whole new view, a darker, more dangerous version of the beauty they'd looked at just hours earlier.

As they followed the valley all the way back to the entrance of Trebah Gardens, Emily felt dread growing inside of her at the thought of uttering the word *goodbye* to her father once more.

CHAPTER NINETEEN

While Daniel and Roy took Chantelle out for another fishing trip on the boat, Emily decided to stay at the cottage to rest and slowly begin the process of packing up their suitcases. The family was leaving England in the morning, something that sat badly on Emily, a weight of grief on her shoulders.

She took a long, lazy bubble bath, trying to hold onto the sense of relaxation she'd discovered in the amazing valley garden, but found it floating away from her, dispersing into the air like dust. Reality always came back to bite at some point or another.

She dressed and spent time styling her hair, watching her own reflection in the bedroom mirror. It was only in these quiet moments that she ever had a chance to put her thoughts together and really work out what she was worried about. She realized now that returning home was bringing two distinct worries into her consciousness; the first being Daniel's potential return to muted enthusiasm over Baby Charlotte; the second was leaving her father.

The whole time they'd been here, she had been worrying about him. The weight loss and his distinct lack of appetite. The coughing fits. The fake smile he adopted for Chantelle's sake that she remembered so distinctly from her childhood. Something wasn't right with him.

Now clean and styled, Emily went into Chantelle's room to begin the task of locating and packing her things. She found the room in a mess, with clothes strewn all over the place, evidence of the flurry of excitement that Chantelle had been in every moment of the vacation. She smiled to herself, glad that the girl had had such a wonderful time, that her mind was filled with happy memories to cherish. Emily's greatest desire when it came to Chantelle was not to repeat the mistakes of her own childhood, to make the girl feel safe and loved at all times, to make her feel special and wanted.

She scooped a summer dress up from the floor and folded it, placing it neatly in the case, then moved onto the next item. As she worked, Emily allowed her thoughts to drift from one thing to the next, letting them flow without direction in order to let the most important ones come to the forefront. And the thought that emerged over and over again in her mind was her father.

She stopped, pausing. The house was empty; she was the only one here. Perhaps she could have a look around the place, see if there was anything that might shed some light on her father's low mood?

She chewed her lip, deliberating. It felt wrong to snoop, like looking in someone's diary. But her father was unlikely to volunteer his concerns to her. Sometimes taking matters into one's own hands was necessary, especially when the means justified the end.

She left Chantelle's room and crossed the corridor to the room that looked like her father's office. She could tell as such due to its unmistakable resemblance to the door of the inn, the one that had remained locked, strictly out of bounds for her and Charlotte. She could still remember the myriad of handprints she and her sister had left on the door while waiting for their father to emerge from his secret lair. Though the handprints were absent on this door, it still gave her that same feeling of being shut out of something, of secrets unuttered.

She tried the doorknob. To her surprise it turned. So her father had not locked this study like he had done the one in the inn. She went inside.

The first thing to strike her about the room was its similarity to his Sunset Harbor office. The furniture was the same, laid out in the same way. It was slightly eerie. A carbon copy of the room he'd had all those years before.

The main difference, however, was all the clocks. They adorned every wall, stood in the windowsill. Roy collected clocks in the same way others collected plants, Emily thought. She herself found the clocks intimidating. Symbolic, even, for the time that was passing from them, the time they had lost, too reminiscent of the finiteness of the time they had left. She shuddered.

Feeling even more uncomfortable with snooping, Emily nevertheless went over to the desk and began looking through her father's stacks of paper. Just like at home, he had piles of insignificant bits of paperwork all over the place. He clearly hadn't found a more efficient system for his hoarding habit.

She thumbed through telephone bills, letters from the water company, a letter from the council about some building plans for the local area. Some of the bits of paper were dated from several years ago. Emily wondered why her father felt the need to hold onto all these things.

She put the bills and letters down, sighing. There was nothing here that may indicate why her father seemed so low at the moment, though she herself would feel weighed down merely by the presence of all these letters, of years' worth of history piled up unnecessarily all over the place.

As she went to leave the office, something caught her eye. On a chair by the door, which she had until now had her back to, there was a box file. Emily thought it unusual for Roy to have one; he wasn't organized enough ordinarily to file some papers away while leaving others strewn about. She went over and pushed the stack of magazines resting on top of the box file to one side.

Looking at the box file filled Emily with dread. She didn't know why, but as she unlatched the lid and pulled it open, she was struck by a horrible emotion, a premonition that there was something inside she wouldn't want to know about.

Her eyes scanned the first document before her, the one lying on the top of the papers contained inside. She gasped, her throat constricting, and staggered back, gripping the desk to keep herself upright. One word and one word only had burned into her vision as she'd looked at the letter addressed to her father: cancer.

She breathed deeply, feeling the world swirl around her. Her heart hammered rapidly. There must be a mistake. She must have read it wrong.

It took all her resolve to look back at the letter, to get to the bottom of it. But it was true. She read it all again, over and over. The letter was from the NHS, and it contained the results of Roy Mitchell's biopsy sample.

It was confirmed.

It was cancer.

CHAPTER TWENTY

Emily's immediate reaction was denial. She could hardly breathe as she searched the letter for a date, not wanting to believe what she had just read, hoping desperately that the letter was from years hence, an old illness he had already beaten during the period they'd been estranged. But no, she saw with horror that the letter was very recent. In fact, it had arrived just before they had. Her father had discovered he had cancer at the very same moment they'd touched down in England. Her heart clenched with agony.

Just then, she heard the front door slam, and the sounds of Chantelle's happy babbling resonated through the house. Emily quickly exited the study, taking the letter with her, and crossed the hall into her room. She lay down on the bed to give the impression she'd been napping.

A moment later, she heard Daniel's footsteps. Then the door opened, light streamed in, and his head appeared around the door.

"Did we wake you?" he asked gently, as she stirred and looked up.

Emily could almost feel the letter burning in her pocket. She so desperately wanted to speak to Daniel about it, but first she needed to speak to her father. So she kept her chin up and her tears in check.

"I've been drifting, that's all," she said. "Did you have a nice time on the boat?"

"It was great. We caught some cod for lunch. Do you think you'll be able to eat any?"

Emily shook her head. Not because of Baby Charlotte, but because of the emotion that was roiling inside of her.

"Too bad," Daniel said. "I'll make you a sandwich instead."

"Thanks," Emily said. "Oh, and Daniel," she added, as he turned toward the door to leave. He looked back. "Can you ask my dad to come up?"

Daniel frowned at the slightly unusual request, but he didn't challenge it. "Sure."

He left the room. Emily felt the pressure of saving face leave her body, and she sagged, exhausted from it. How had her father managed to keep his secret during the whole holiday when she could barely even get through one conversation without cracking from the strain?

She sat up and rubbed her rounded stomach. She'd been on such a high with the pregnancy, but now, after having read the letter, she felt desperately sad. Would her father be around to meet Baby Charlotte? The thought of him dying turned her bones to ice.

There was a soft knock on the door, and Roy peered around. Emily smiled sadly at him.

"Is everything okay?" Roy asked. "Daniel said you weren't feeling able to eat cod for lunch."

Emily remained silent. She couldn't utter any words. Seeing her father now it seemed as plain as day that he was sick. In fact, she became aware that she'd known subconsciously from the very first moment she'd seen his face over FaceTime. She just hadn't wanted to allow herself to believe it.

Instead of saying anything, Emily took the letter out of her pocket and handed it to Roy. His face blanched when he saw what she had discovered.

"Oh," he said, simply, sitting down on the bed beside her. His posture looked completely defeated.

"I don't know what to say," Emily managed, her voice cracking through her tears.

Roy looked at her, his expression mirroring hers. He cupped her cheeks in his hands, and her tears streamed over his wizened fingers.

"My darling," he said, his voice cracking too. He began to sob.

Emily gripped his hands where they lay against her cheeks. Her heart heaved.

"Dad, you need to come back to America with us. There are amazing doctors over there, much more choices. No matter what it costs we will find you the best specialist."

"Emily Jane..." Roy said softly, the protest in his voice audible.

"No," Emily insisted. "I won't hear anything about you thinking you're putting me out, or wanting to be independent. Your health is far more important than pride. I can make some calls now."

She went to stand but felt Roy's hand touch hers, urging her to sit and listen. She looked back and saw the expression in her father's eyes. She half fell, half sat, landing back on the mattress heavily, a pressure of realization settling on her chest.

"Dad," she managed to say. "Is it going to be okay?"

Her voice sounded like a child's. A memory came back to Emily then, of her and Roy in this very same position after a particularly horrendous fight with Patricia. She'd asked the same question. *Are you leaving? Is it going to be okay?* And he had lied. He'd said he wasn't going anywhere. He'd promised things were going to be okay. But they hadn't been. He'd left, tearing a hole in her life that had only just begun to heal.

This time, Roy didn't lie. He didn't put on his fake smile or his jovial voice—the one he'd used when she was young, the one he'd used with Chantelle all week. This time, he just shook his head.

"I've seen the best specialists," he told her calmly. "I have had second, third, and fourth opinions. There is nothing that can be done."

Emily's heart broke. The pain was real, visceral, like nothing she'd ever felt before. She clutched her chest as a sob racked through her.

Roy's arms were around her in an instant. On the bed they held each other and wept for what felt like an eternity. Emily had never felt grief like it. Even in the darkest times of her youth when she had no idea whether Roy was dead or alive she had never felt anything like this. Even after losing Charlotte, because she had no ability to understand then what the years of grief would feel like, what toll the loss would take on her. But now she knew. Now she had experience. She had lived without Charlotte. She had lost Trevor. She knew all too well the pain losing her father would unleash upon her.

"Do you know how long you have left?" Emily finally managed to say. She didn't want to know the answer but at the same time felt compelled to know, to have all the facts.

Roy's embrace tightened in response. She could feel his body shaking with emotion as it pressed against hers, his bones more pronounced than ever.

"A year," he whispered. "At most."

Emily's breath came in short, panicked puffs. This was unreal. This wasn't happening. Her world was shattering around her.

"You have to come back to Sunset Harbor with us," Emily stammered. "I can't leave you here alone. We have plenty of room, we can make you comfortable."

But Roy shook his head. In a kind, polite, yet firm voice, Roy said, "Emily Jane, I can't. My life is here."

"But what am I going to do without you?" she gasped.

Roy's voice sounded in her ear, affirmative and confident. "You're going to do what you did before. You're going to live a rich, full, successful life, filled with happiness and joy."

Emily shook her head. There was no way. Losing her father so soon after finding him was the cruelest blow that fate had ever dealt her. She wanted to scream at the sky for burdening her with a life so filled with misery. Was there never to be an end to her agony?

But it was Daniel's words that came to her mind, that things do happen for a reason, that it may not feel like it at the time but every experience is to teach us a lesson.

She finally moved from Roy's embrace and looked at him. He seemed so small, so fragile. She realized then that the tables had turned. She'd been desperate for him to return to her and parent her in a way he'd failed to do in her young adult years. But now she could see that he needed her. She had to be the caregiver, the soother. Fate had brought them back together so she could care for Roy in his final months of life. It was time for her to step up and take control. To put her emotions aside for his benefit, as he had done for her after every fight with Patricia.

Wiping the last tear from her eye, Emily took both of his hands in hers, filled with a maternal sense of protectiveness.

"We can't tell Chantelle," she said.

He nodded in agreement.

She continued. "I will speak to Daniel once we're home."

Roy nodded again. He seemed relieved that the decisions had been taken out of his hands. His secret must have been weighing on him so much.

"And we're buying you a phone," Emily added with finality. "We're speaking every single day from this point forward. We are going to write a lifetime's worth of letters and postcards to each other. You are going to do all the things you were always too afraid to do and you're going to send me photos of all of it. You're going to travel the world. You're going to document everything. Okay?"

Through his sorrow, Emily saw Roy's face brighten and lift.

"You want your old man to join the amateur dramatics group at last?" he said, still able to find his humor in the darkness of the moment.

"You're going to be in the Christmas play," Emily confirmed. "And you're sending me a video of the whole thing."

Roy smiled. Emily felt a surge of confidence, of responsibility. To take any fear and unhappiness away from Roy was her new goal.

She smiled back. Fate seemed to want to knock her back at every opportunity, but she was not going to let it defeat her.

CHAPTER TWENTY ONE

"I wish we didn't have to go home today," Chantelle said sadly, looking up from her clock pieces.

The family was sat at the dining table in the kitchen, half eating breakfast, half occupied in a variety of activities—Emily reading a book, Daniel a newspaper, and Chantelle and Roy their clock fixing. The child had become something of a expert at clock fixing, something Roy put down to her "nimble little fingers" and eagerness to learn.

"I know," Daniel said to her. "It's gone by so quickly. But it will be nice to see Mogsy and Rain again, won't it?"

Chantelle nodded. "And the chickens."

"It's been wonderful, Dad," Emily added, echoing their sentiments.

Roy nodded, giving her a knowing look that Emily knew neither Daniel nor Chantelle would be able to understand or even notice.

Emily nibbled her plain waffle, filled with sadness. Roy had made them a feast for their final breakfast—a fry-up. There were stacks of different items, from beans to waffles, bacon to toast, scrambled eggs and fried eggs and poached eggs. Emily was just about able to sample a little bit of everything, but she did so with a heavy heart.

"Is everything packed?" Roy asked then.

Emily looked over at their cases lined up by the door and nodded. She desperately wanted to stay, particularly with the heart-breaking news of her father's cancer diagnosis. But she also felt a sense of calm and strength now that she was taking on the parental role in their relationship. Something had shifted in her. The goodbye that was to soon be forced upon them by fate had changed her. She didn't need Roy to parent her anymore or make up for lost time. She was strong, independent. Her role now was to love him to her maximum ability and make sure he lived his final months filled with happiness.

They finished their breakfast and tidied up. Then there was nothing left to do but load Roy's car.

As she climbed into the back seat beside Chantelle, Emily took one last lingering look at her father's house. She would be back, she knew that much, but it still felt so poignant. When she'd arrived here she'd thought they had the luxury of decades of years stretching ahead of them. But that had been taken from her, cut back to just a dozen months. The number of times she would look upon this house was fewer than she could ever have realized.

In the front seat, Daniel and Roy discussed sailing and boat care, chatting happily like the dear friends they were. Emily felt a pit of sadness in her stomach knowing she would be breaking the news to Daniel once they returned to Maine. Then she glanced at Chantelle. Roy's impending death would devastate her more than anyone. She loved her Papa Roy. He was her hero. That fate would take him away from Emily was cruel enough, but to take him from Chantelle when she so desperately needed adult role models and long-lasting loving relationships was a tragedy.

Emily fell into silence as she watched the world go by. The summer sun had vanished behind a layer of clouds today, and there was cold moisture in the air that hinted at rain. The weather had been so perfect while they'd been in England but now on the day they were leaving they were getting a small insight into the dreary weather the country was famed for.

As they reached the airport, the rain began to fall. Daniel grabbed their cases from the trunk, racing them out of the rain and inside the building. Then he returned for Chantelle and grabbed her hand. They raced inside.

Emily, on the other hand, felt no need to rush. The drizzle on her face felt cleansing. Roy, too, seemed serene as she looped her arm through his. They strolled together, neither in a rush, across the parking lot and into the building.

Chantelle laughed when she saw them. "Mommy, your hair has gone all frizzy. And Papa Roy, look at your suit."

The old man glanced at the shoulders of his brown jacket that were now streaked dark with rain. "I am used to it," he remarked, smiling.

Chantelle threw her arms around him then. "I'm going to miss you!" she exclaimed.

Emily watched on, her chest heavy with emotion. Roy and Chantelle embraced for a long, long time. As they did, Emily saw Chantelle transform into Charlotte. Another memory of another time, of a goodbye she had long ago forgotten. Then they let each other go, and it was Chantelle she saw again.

Daniel and Roy embraced next. The affection they showed one another warmed Emily. They never felt any qualms about hugging in public, never showed any manly displays of awkward handshakes and back slaps. She smiled at them.

Finally, it was Emily's turn. The moment she'd been dreading had arrived.

She held her father's arms, just above the elbows, and looked deeply into his eyes. He adopted the same position. Something unspoken passed between them, an unconditional love, unique to them, that only they could understand and communicate.

Roy's eyes grew red and tears began to trickle down his cheeks. In response, Emily allowed her own tears to fall.

"We'll see each other again soon," Roy said, his grip on Emily's arms tightening.

Emily couldn't help but wonder whether they would, whether soon to her father meant something entirely different than it did to her. And anyway, she had instructed her father to enjoy every moment of his final months of life. He should be jetting off to Paris, not planning a trip to the inn.

"Perhaps," she said, a small smile tugging at the corner of her lips. "Or maybe you'll be too busy surfing in Auckland, swimming with dolphins, scuba diving and paragliding." She shrugged playfully.

Roy's tears continued to flow, but his face cracked into a smile.

They hugged, holding each other as tightly as possible, so close it was almost painful. Emily had never felt so close to her father. It was as if his diagnosis had entirely eradicated any of her feelings of abandonment. There was no time now for her to hold onto any ill feeling toward him. There was nothing to be gained by holding onto it any longer. Every last unconscious ounce of resentment she'd ever felt left her body. She felt free. Light. A sense of clarity overcame her. A sense of gratitude.

As her heart beat against her father's she channeled her forgiveness into him. When they released each other and gazed once more into one another's eyes, Emily knew that he understood. He had no need to feel guilt anymore. The past was forgiven; it was over. There was only the future now. And it was precious.

She saw the change in his eyes as well. The weight he had carried around his neck like an albatross all those years, the guilt, the regret, all of it left him.

Emily took a step back. Her arms fell from her father. His fell too as she stepped back again. Their gaze was locked. Then Emily grinned. Roy grinned too, his entire face lighting up.

Emily turned on her heel, away from Roy and toward her family. She knew she would not look back at her father. Because if she never saw him again, that was the last memory she wanted of him.

Forgiven.

Unburdened.

Loved.

Happy.

CHAPTER TWENTY TWO

The flight home was a bumpy, uncomfortable one. After hitting a pocket of turbulence, Baby Charlotte made her unhappiness known by making Emily throw up several times. Chantelle grew more irritable with every hour that passed. Emily assumed it was because she was upset about leaving Papa Roy, but she projected it at everything else—the movie being boring, the food not being tasty, there being no interesting pictures left to do in her coloring book. She whined and complained the whole time, and Daniel grew exhausted trying to keep her entertained.

By the time they landed in Maine, Emily was thoroughly fed up. She was parched from a combination of dehydration, vomiting, and breathing the airplane's recycled air. Unlike the journey out, she'd been so preoccupied with her thoughts she hadn't managed to sleep at all, and so she was weary as well as nauseous. Adding Chantelle's bad mood to the mix, and her nerves were frayed.

Their bags took forever to appear on the carousel, during which time Chantelle needed the toilet, then complained of hunger, then needed the toilet once again. Daniel and Emily took it in turns to tend to her, but Emily was finding herself growing increasingly close to snapping. It wasn't often either she or Daniel scolded Chantelle but her behavior since leaving England seemed to be deteriorating.

They carried their cases through the airport. Chantelle's strap broke and she tumbled to the floor, hitting her knee and elbow. She let out a bloodcurdling howl and lay sprawled in the middle of the floor.

Emily buried her face in her hands. This was too much. Last time Chantelle had had to say goodbye to Papa Roy she'd had a meltdown. If she was going to act like the world had fallen in on her every time she had to say goodbye then how on earth was she going to get over his death? Emily shook the unpleasant thoughts from her mind and gritted her teeth. She heaved up Chantelle's bag and then looked over her shoulder at Daniel. He was laden with cases.

"Can you help her?" she asked.

Daniel looked tired enough to collapse. He shot her an appealing glance but Emily wasn't backing down. She didn't have the patience right now to deal with a Chantelle tantrum.

Thankfully, Daniel stepped up to the task. He went over to Chantelle and soothed her without paying too much attention to her overexaggeration. He rubbed her elbow briskly.

"There, all better," he said.

Chantelle kept wailing but Daniel paid her no further attention, instead taking her by the hand and leading her gently along, trying to distract her by pointing out stores and all the American brands that they hadn't seen for a week. Emily sighed, relieved the situation had been at least partly resolved.

Out in the parking lot, they found their car and heaved all of the heavy bags into the trunk.

"I'll need to stop for coffee," Daniel said as he got into the driver's seat. "I'm exhausted."

From the passenger seat beside him, Emily touched his arm, communicating both sympathy and affection. In her car seat in the back, Chantelle continued to whine.

Daniel started up the truck and drove them out of the airport parking lot. The traffic was very heavy and they almost immediately got into a slow-moving queue of cars.

"How long will it take us to get home?" Chantelle asked, her voice morose.

"Well, we're currently going the same speed as an old lady on a bicycle," Daniel said, wryly. "So hopefully in time for you to start college."

Emily smirked, but as she looked at Chantelle in the rearview mirror, she saw the child was not impressed with her father's joke. She really was in a foul mood.

"I'd better call the inn," Emily said. "Let them know we're running late."

She used her cell phone to dial the inn's number. It rang for a long time before finally being answered by a voice she couldn't immediately place.

"Who's that?" Emily asked, confused.

"Emily? It's Bryony."

Emily frowned. Why was Bryony on reception? "Where's Lois?" she asked.

There was a hesitation. Then Bryony said, "She's just dealing with a guest at the moment. There was a bit of a problem with a double booking."

Emily's frown grew deeper. "How?" she asked. "The booking system is all automatic thanks to your form. Shouldn't double booking be impossible?"

Another pause. "About that…" Bryony began, sounding guilty. "I kinda accidentally didn't take down a test page that I'd made and there was still a link to it on the main site, so a couple of people booked through that page and we didn't have a record of them coming, although we did take their money."

Emily was too stunned to speak. It took her a while to formulate a composed response. "How many is a couple?"

"Like, the whole third floor..."

Emily breathed deeply. "So twenty rooms in the inn have been double booked."

Beside her, she saw Daniel's face turn sharply to look at her with surprise. She closed her eyes, trying to stay calm.

"Yeah," Bryony confirmed. "Lois is dealing with it now. A couple of people turned up who we had to turn away, but the rest are for later in the year so it's just a case of calling them to cancel and arrange the refunds. Which I've volunteered to do because it was my error. Hence being on reception."

Emily rubbed her exhausted eyes. This was the last thing she needed. In the seat behind her, she could hear Chantelle complaining of being hungry. Ahead of her was nothing but a row of red brake lights, stretching as far as the eye could see. So much for holding onto her holiday relaxation.

"Okay. Well, look, we're running late because of the traffic. So can you and Lois just sort this out before I get back? I can't be dealing with this right now." She hung up and looked at Daniel. "You heard that, right?"

"Yeah. But how did that even happen?"

"A website glitch," Emily explained, not bothering to go into too much detail.

The drive home took forever. By the time they turned into the driveway of the inn, everyone was in as equally foul a mood as the other.

The parking lot was full—Emily remembered there was a wedding reception booked in the ballroom that evening—so Daniel parked the pickup truck round the back. They got their suitcases out, and Emily realized with wry amusement that they looked like very grumpy guests arriving for a vacation none of them wanted.

They went inside. A few drunken wedding guests were milling about in the hallway, one or two smoking cigarettes out of the open French doors in the lounge. Discarded wine glasses were all over the place from people who'd been passing through.

"Please, no smoking inside," Emily told them.

They guiltily stubbed out their cigarettes.

She found Lois on the reception desk. When Lois looked up and saw Emily she tried to smile brightly, but Emily could see straight through it.

Lois opened her mouth to speak but Emily held up a hand to stop her.

"I spoke to Bryony," she said. "So I already know. And I'm too tired to deal with it right now so please just tell me it's all sorted."

"It's all sorted," Lois said. "Only the double booking isn't the only problem."

Emily closed her eyes and took a deep breath. She looked at Daniel quickly. "Can you get Chantelle some dinner, please?" He nodded, then as soon as they were gone, she turned back to the matter at hand. Bracing herself, she asked, "Okay. What is it?"

Lois took a deep breath as though she was about to launch into a very long story. "The catering company for the wedding party has been stuck in traffic all day. So the bride has no food or drink and she's kinda hysterical. I was going to open up the speakeasy but Alec can't do a shift tonight so I've just taken all the wine and liquor from there and put it in the ballroom."

Emily grimaced. It would be at huge cost to them but at least Lois had found a solution. "What about Parker and Matthew? Can they make up some finger foods?"

"They're both busy doing the dinner shift."

Emily grabbed the phone and sent a mass text out to her friends. *SOS. I have a hysterical bride and no caterers. If anyone can spare an hour making hors d'oeurves I will be eternally grateful.*

Then she looked back up at Lois. "Okay, I've put out a call for help. Now where's the bride?"

"Last time I saw her she was wandering the grounds crying. She won't talk to anyone, not even the groom."

Emily nodded. She was in full-on problem-solving mode. She went outside and walked the length of the lawns, searching for the bride. She found her, finally, right down at the end of the yard by the rose bushes, weeping bitterly. The bottom of her beautiful lace gown was stained with mud.

Emily introduced herself. "I'm the manager here," she explained. "I hear things aren't going according to plan today."

The bride looked inconsolable. "The traffic's held up my food and half my guests!" she wailed. "There was supposed to be a jazz band playing but most of them are sick and didn't turn up."

Emily thought of Owen's band. They'd become a staple of the inn now, and played most weekends. If wedding parties wanted them for the reception they could be included in the hire fee for the ballroom at a discounted price. She would have to get to the bottom of that.

"I'm going to solve this," Emily told her.

She went back inside and called Serena.

"Is Owen sick?" she asked her friend.

"Food poisoning," Serena confirmed. "I've got it too. We were all out last night and must have had something bad. I'm sorry, Lois called earlier frantic for some help but I can't even get out of bed."

Emily finished the call with Serena, exasperated, unsure how to resolve the situation. They could set up a laptop and connect it to the speakers, but the wedding was supposed to have live music and it wouldn't be quite the same. She wondered then if she could call on Roman. He was supposed to be a friend, maybe he'd be willing to help her out of a sticky situation? She dialed his number.

"Do you think you could do a surprise gig tonight?" she asked. "Only an hour. I have a weeping bride expecting live music but only the double bass player and drummer are well enough to perform."

Roman seemed to see the humor in the situation. "I'll do it," he laughed.

"Really?" Emily asked, amazed. "Are you sure?"

"I'm part of the community now," Roman replied. "I want to do my part. I'll be right over."

Emily sighed with relief. All would be forgiven when none other than Roman Westbrook arrived to perform at the reception! Even having a laptop play music for the rest of the evening would be more readily tolerated.

With that ticked off the list, Emily checked her phone to see whether anyone had replied to her appeal. There was a message from Karen saying she'd just baked a batch of cheese straws and was on her way over with them. Cynthia had also replied saying she and her son, Jeremy, were in the area anyway on a bike ride and were happy to stop by and help. Before she had a chance to hit reply and thank them, she heard the sound of car doors slamming outside. She went and looked out and saw Raj and Sunita coming out of their car.

"We got your message," Sunita said, trotting up the steps toward her. "How can we help?"

Emily hugged them both in turn. "Can you head into the kitchen? See what we have that could be made into a buffet?"

They nodded and hurried off inside. Just then, she saw Cynthia and Jeremy riding along the driveway. Emily sighed with relief. People had responded to her so quickly and she was beyond grateful. She guided them to the kitchen also. Then finally Karen arrived with her baskets of breadsticks and cheese straws. Emily went into the kitchen with her to see how things were going.

Inside, the room was in utter chaos. Matthew and Parker were rushed off their feet trying to make all the meals for the dinner shift of a fully booked inn. Marnie was running around with plates. Daniel and Chantelle were nowhere to be seen, and Emily assumed that the moment Daniel had caught sight of the chaos he'd whisked Chantelle away without dinner. Wonderful. She'd have a hungry, grumpy child on her hands once all of this was resolved.

Sunita, Raj, Jeremy, and Cynthia were busy toasting bagels, cutting them into bite-sized pieces and slathering them with cream cheese and smoked salmon.

"I'll roast these potatoes and fill them with cheese and chives," Karen said, grabbing produce from the fridge.

It wasn't much, but it was better than nothing. Emily helped prepare the food with them, then they tried to make it look as presentable as possible by putting it on silver trays. They carried them through to the ballroom, setting the food up on the empty banquet tables.

Inside the ballroom, Emily could see why the bride was so unhappy. It wasn't even half full. The drummer and double bass player from the band were improvising music on the corner stage, but no one was dancing.

Emily felt so bad for the bride. This was supposed to be her perfect day. She thought of her own wonderful wedding and vowed to do all she could to make it up to her. But it was so overwhelming. She felt as if everything at the inn had fallen apart in her absence.

At least the guests seemed grateful that there was now food. As they came over to get some, Roman walked in.

"Thank God you're here," Emily said to him.

He tipped his fedora and then leapt onto the stage with his characteristic swagger. Guests began gasping as they realized who it was standing there.

Roman repositioned the microphone next to the piano where Owen usually sat. He conferred with the other two band members, then counted to three, and they began to play a poppy jazz number, a real toe tapper. Thankfully, people began to dance.

The bride must have been able to hear the music from the lawns because she emerged into the ballroom moments later. At the sight of her guests dancing, plates of food in their hands, a small smile spread to her lips. Then when she saw Roman Westbrook singing and playing piano on the stage her mouth dropped open. She looked at Emily, flabbergasted.

"I hope this goes some way in making up for things," Emily said to her.

The bride was too stunned to speak. She just nodded. The groom came over and took her by the hand, leading her to the dance floor to finally begin the party.

Emily sighed with relief and ushered her friends out of the room.

"Thanks so much, guys," she told them all. "You're actual life savers."

But before she had a chance to wish them all goodbye, she heard a ruckus coming from the dining room. She peered inside just in time to see Marnie burst into tears. The girl came flying out of the room.

Emily stopped her in her tracks, taking her by the shoulders. All around, her friends looked concerned for her.

"What happened?" Emily asked.

"It's that Professor Vaughn!" Marnie wailed. "He booked the carriage house for a fortnight. He's only been here for three days but all he does it complain. I can't stand it anymore. He's so rude."

Emily remembered the carriage house being booked by the mysterious Mr. X. It had turned out to be a professor, not the Bond villain she'd jokingly hypothesized at the time. Although by the way Marnie was carrying on, it sounded like he was a villain of sorts.

"Let me handle him," Emily said. "You go and take a minute to compose yourself, okay?"

Marnie scurried off and Emily went into the dining room. Mr. X, aka Professor Vaughn, was immediately recognizable. He had a large, angry red face and his table was in disarray, half eaten dishes discarded and left haphazardly all over it. He had guests with him, other fuming arrogant professor types. All around them, the other diners were giving them the side eye. Emily used her most calm, professional voice.

"Professor Vaughn?" she asked.

He frowned at her. "Who the hell are you?"

"I'm the manager," she said. "I understand things aren't to your satisfaction this evening."

"The soup is cold," he complained.

Emily kept her face neutral. "It's gazpacho soup," she explained. "It is traditionally served chilled."

"I don't give two hoots about your tradition," Professor Vaughn barked. "Can't you see I'm entertaining academics? We want our food hot. And we want our drinks. We've been waiting ages."

"What drinks did you order?" Emily asked, remaining as neutral as ever. "I'll see if I can get them sent out immediately."

"Wine," Professor Vaughn replied shortly.

Emily breathed deeply and left the dining room. No wonder Marnie was so upset. If he'd behaved that way for three days over everything she'd be close to tears as well.

She went into the kitchen. "Does anyone know what happened to Professor Vaughn's wine?" she asked.

"Lois had to divert all the wine to the wedding party," Matthew explained. "We told him there was no wine but he wouldn't accept it."

Emily chewed her lip. Just then, she heard the sound of a van coming around to park at the back of the inn. She looked out and to her relief saw the wedding party's catering van had finally arrived.

The men started bringing crates into the already crowded kitchen. It was all hands on deck to get the food onto plates and out into the ballroom. Raj hurried out of the room with his arms filled with wine bottles. From the open crate, Emily grabbed some bottles. She carried them into the dining room and presented one to Professor Vaughn.

"What did I say to that silly little waitress?" he barked to the other academics. "I knew there had to be wine somewhere. She obviously wasn't looking hard enough."

Swallowing her irritation, Emily went to the other tables of diners. She put the other bottles of wine upon them.

"These are on the house," she said under her breath so Professor Vaughn couldn't hear. "An apology for the unsavory company you've all been subjected to." She smiled sweetly.

The other diners seemed quite pleased with their free wine. Emily also turned some music on in the room so that his loud conversation wasn't quite so apparent for everyone.

Satisfied the situation had finally been resolved, Emily finished helping the caterers for the wedding. Then she bade farewell to her friends, thanking them profusely for all their help. Thanks to them, they had narrowly averted disaster.

Weary, her head pounding, Emily went upstairs to find Daniel. He wasn't in their room, so she checked Chantelle's. Again, it was empty.

Confused, she decided to look in the nursery. To her surprise, she found them both inside. But rather than the half decorated, sparsely furnished room it had been before the vacation, some items had been delivered in their absence, including a toy box and a collection of books. And they were all now strewn about the room. In the middle of it all, Chantelle was weeping bitterly.

Daniel looked up at Emily, his eyes filled with apologies.

"She's been tantruming this whole time?" Emily asked, exasperated.

Daniel just nodded. "I think it's almost run its course."

Emily sunk into the nursing chair that Amy had bought her. She was so tired she could easily fall asleep, but Chantelle's bitter tears were too loud. Daniel shuffled over and rested his head on her knees. She stroked his hair tenderly.

"Chantelle," Emily said, gazing up at the ceiling. "Can you tell me what's wrong? Why did you trash the baby's things?"

"Because I hate her!" Chantelle roared.

Emily knew she didn't mean it. She was having a meltdown over Roy. It was all bubbling up now and she was taking it out on the baby.

"I hate that she gets a nice room and books and toys!" Chantelle screeched again. "And I hate that she gets you as her mommy when I had to have Sheila. It's not fair!"

Seeing her raw pain hurt Emily. She wished she could take it away but all she could do was support Chantelle through these moments.

"You're right," she said. "It's not fair."

Chantelle stopped and looked up, surprised.

"But blaming the baby won't help. What will help is talking, and crying if you need to, and snuggling up in bed with me and Daddy and watching movies, drawing pictures, then talking some more." She stood and held her hand out to Chantelle. "I don't know about you, but watching movies in bed is way more fun than lying on the floor surrounded by mess."

Chantelle ignored the hand that was extended to her, but she did get up off the floor and waltz out of the room. Emily watched as she stomped along the corridor and into the master bedroom.

Daniel let out a deep sigh. "You can work miracles with that girl," he said.

"Maybe. Or maybe I've just set us up for an entire evening of tantrums."

He stood and helped her out of the stool. Arm in arm, they walked into the master bedroom to see just what Chantelle had in store for them that night.

CHAPTER TWENTY THREE

The next morning, over breakfast, Emily checked her calendar and saw that she had an appointment scheduled with Doctor Arkwright that she had completely forgotten about. It had been booked long before the last-minute vacation to England and had slipped her mind entirely. An appointment after a long flight, a crazy evening of work, jet lag, and a poor night's sleep in the company of a grumpy child wasn't exactly ideal.

"I'm sorry it's such short notice," Emily said to Daniel. "You'll be able to get the time off work though?"

He looked less than pleased, and rubbed the frown line between his eyebrows with exasperation. "There's so much to catch up on, what with Jack being off injured. I'm overseeing the whole thing now. They need me onsite."

Emily felt crushed. "I thought you wanted to come to every appointment," she said, dejected.

"And I do," Daniel said, his tone slightly snappy. "I'm not working this hard out of choice. If I could I'd prioritize the baby."

Emily narrowed her eyes. She couldn't help but feel as though he were taking a swipe at her for laying too much work on his shoulders.

"What do you mean by that?" she asked.

Daniel sighed and stood from the table, taking his empty coffee mug with him. He dumped it in the sink. "I just mean I'm busy right now. That's all. But I will get the time off. You know I will. I always do."

Emily watched, exasperated, as he left the room. While she appreciated that he was extra busy with the renovation work now that Jack was injured, his attitude left a lot to be desired. It certainly didn't help her sense of anxiety over what Daniel truly felt about the baby. What was worse was the way she'd had a premonition about this, that once the vacation was over and they returned to their normal life Daniel would go back to acting stressed whenever she brought up the baby.

Sadly, she ate her toast, sitting alone at the kitchen table. She wished her father was here. Even her mother would do right now, just to alleviate the loneliness Daniel's dramatic exit had stirred in her. It was too early in the morning to call Roy; it would still be nighttime in England. She scrolled down her list of contacts to her mom's. She stared at it for a while, before sighing and putting her phone away. Now wasn't the time to speak to Patricia. But then again, Emily thought, when would be? Her mom still didn't know she was going to be a grandmother. The thought of telling her caused anxiety to swirl in her stomach. As if in response, she felt the familiar butterfly sensation of Baby Charlotte.

"Sorry, sweetheart," she whispered to her stomach.

As she did so, it occurred to her that she wasn't alone, not really. Not while Charlotte grew inside of her. The thought was comforting.

Daniel came back into the kitchen then. "Okay, I've called the contractors to say I won't be onsite until after lunch. Are you ready?"

His tone was short. Emily almost wanted to retort that she didn't need him to come, but she knew she was being childish.

Instead, she stood and gathered her purse.

They went out through the corridor, and Emily could hear Professor Vaughn in the dining room complaining loudly over the consistency of his fried egg as they passed.

Out in the parking lot, they got into Daniel's pickup truck. He was silent, his expression dark as he drove them along the driveway and out onto the street.

Emily looked glumly out the window at Trevor's house as they passed. The lawn was filled with the machinery needed to redo the garden, though there was no one currently onsite to operate it. She tried to remind herself that managing both projects must be very stressful for Daniel, but at the same time she didn't think it was fair for him to take it out on her, or make her feel so worried about whether he even wanted the baby or not.

They didn't speak the entire drive to Doctor Arkwright's. Daniel seemed completely lost in his thoughts.

"Careful, that light's turning red," Emily said when she thought he wasn't paying enough attention.

"I can see that," he replied tersely, slowing the truck to a halt at the traffic signal.

Emily felt herself grow even more irritated with him.

They reached the office and Daniel parked in the lot. As they walked across to the doors, Emily caught him checking his phone.

Considering Daniel usually was awful with technology it was extra infuriating to her that he would be preoccupied with it now.

The receptionist signed them in on the computer and directed them to one of the rooms down the hall. Emily felt far more at ease in the medical environment now, though not completely without anxiety. The smell still bothered her, with its clinicalness that reminded her of the time when Trevor passed away. Thinking about Trevor set of a chain reaction of thoughts in her mind, leading her to her father, to the fact she was soon to lose him too. Unhappiness seemed to crowd in at her from all sides like a black cloud of despair.

Doctor Arkwright entered and Emily's gaze snapped up. She shook her hand and greeted her in her kind yet efficient manner.

"How has it all been going?" she asked, taking her seat.

Emotion threatened to choke Emily. She swallowed and forced her mind away from the darkness. "It's been fine," she said. "The morning sickness is a bit relentless."

"That's normal," Doctor Arkwright said, "though unpleasant. Eat blander foods if possible and make sure you're staying hydrated after you're sick." She turned and read some notes off her computer. "Okay, so we're here for some blood tests."

"We are?" Emily said, surprised. She hadn't realized that was what the appointment was for.

"Yes, this is the quadruple test," Doctor Arkwright said. "It's to measure certain proteins and hormones in your blood which might indicate that your baby has genetic abnormalities."

Emily felt her face drain of warmth. How had this slipped her mind? How had she not even been thinking about this test? She'd gotten too ahead of herself with excitement. She hadn't even had the full range of tests yet to make sure Charlotte was healthy.

"What happens if there's something wrong with her?" Emily asked, hearing her voice tremble. She looked over at Daniel, feeling fearful. By his expression she concluded he didn't share the same fears as her.

"You'd be offered an amniocentesis diagnostic test," the doctor explained. "But we're getting a little ahead of ourselves. Let's just draw your blood first, shall we?"

Emily presented her arm for Doctor Arkwright, who cleaned her inner elbow with antiseptic and prepared the needle.

"How long will the results take to come in?" Emily asked, wincing as the needle slid into her arm.

"About a week," the doctor replied.

A week seemed like a very long time for Emily to stew on the results of such an important test. She looked up at Daniel to see that he was frowning at his phone.

"Can you please pay attention?" she snapped across the office at him.

The atmosphere in the room changed instantly. Daniel looked up. Even Doctor Arkwright tensed.

"It's Lois," Daniel replied. "The contractors haven't shown up."

Emily wanted to scream at him, "So what?" How could he even care about contractors at a time like this! How could he care more about the renovations at Trevor's house than his pregnant wife? But she didn't. She bit her lip and focused on the sharp pain of the needle drawing her blood.

"All done," Doctor Arkwright said.

She sat back down and scribbled labels onto each of the four vials of blood she'd taken from Emily. At the sight of them, Emily felt instantly woozy. She rubbed her forehead. It felt clammy.

Doctor Arkwright observed her, a slight frown on her head. "Are you feeling faint, Emily?" she asked.

Emily nodded, the world swirling as she did.

"Let me take your blood pressure."

Doctor Arkwright attached the cuff to Emily's arm and started the machine. Emily felt an unpleasant squeezing sensation in her upper arm that grew tighter and tighter. Then finally there was a bleep and the pressure was released.

Doctor Arkwright studied the little slip of paper that printed out of the machine. "Hmm, your blood pressure is a little low for my liking."

"Is that bad?"

"Not necessarily," the doctor explained. "It's certainly very common. Make sure you're drinking lots of fluids and you could increase your salt intake a little. And of course, make sure you're taking things easy." She leaned forward in her chair then, looking Emily straight in the eye. "How are your stress levels?"

Emily knew that she was referring to the fact she'd just barked at Daniel. She felt embarrassed that he'd put her in such a position, made her give off the wrong impression to the doctor.

"Work has been a bit difficult recently," Emily confessed.

"Anything else that might be worth noting?" Doctor Arkwright pressed.

Emily felt very under scrutiny. The doctor must be able to see the stress and anxiety radiating from her. She desperately wanted to mention the stress of her father's cancer diagnosis but she hadn't yet found the time to tell Daniel and now definitely was not it.

"Life is always hectic," Emily replied. "I'll try to slow down a bit."

The doctor nodded. "Right, well, I think it would be best to have you back in next week for the blood test results."

"Is that necessary?" Emily asked. "Can't you give them over the phone?"

"I can, but I'd like to keep a closer eye on your blood pressure anyway," the doctor explained.

It just made Emily feel even more worried. Doctor Arkwright was keeping a closer eye on her than would be usual. It made her squirm uncomfortably.

The doctor booked a follow-up appointment and then wished Emily and Daniel goodbye. As they walked out, Emily felt like a bag of nerves. The appointment had done little to reassure her. If anything, it had compounded her stress.

She turned to Daniel to offload but saw his phone pressed up to his ear. Whatever call he was making must have connected because he started speaking, and Emily heard him leaving an angry message for the contractors who'd failed to show up. Emily couldn't believe it. He'd barely even left the doctor's office before getting back to work.

"Daniel, please," Emily snapped the second he hung up. "I'm stressing out here about the baby and it's like you're not even there."

"I'm sorry," Daniel replied, exasperated, and to Emily's ears he sounded anything but. "You know what it's like. Sometimes you have to drop everything for work, too."

Emily stared at him, mouth agape. Where had the gentle man who rubbed her back when she was sick gone? Why had he been replaced by this stressed-out grump?

Silently, she got back into the passenger's seat. As Daniel reversed out of the lot, she turned her face so he could not see the tear trickling down her cheek.

Not that he'd notice it anyway, she thought bitterly.

*

They returned home just as Yvonne's car was pulling out of the drive. She waved at them both, Bailey in the passenger seat waving also. Emily wound down her window.

"Was Chantelle good today?" she called out, a little worried about the child's behavior following her most recent meltdown.

"She was a pleasure as always," Yvonne replied. "She fixed my clock! Said Papa Roy taught her how! Anyway, we're in a hurry for ballet lessons. Lois is there so I just dropped Chantelle with her. Is that okay?"

"Of course, of course," Emily said.

Yvonne waved goodbye and drove on. Daniel parked outside the inn.

"I'm heading over to Trevor's," he said.

He kissed Emily lightly, but she didn't feel the usual warmth and care she normally would. She was still too angry.

"See you for dinner," she said, a little pointedly.

She went inside the inn and looked around. The reception desk was empty. No Lois in sight.

"Chantelle?" Emily called out.

There was no response.

Just then, Lois came hurrying down the steps, her arms filled with towels. "Sorry, Professor Vaughn demanded new towels. He said the last batch weren't clean enough." She rolled her eyes.

"It's fine," Emily said. "But where's Chantelle? I thought you were keeping an eye on her."

"She went to the conservatory to read," Lois said.

Emily frowned. "Alone? She's seven years old and this house is full of guests. She needs to be supervised at all times."

She could hear her tone, snappy. She was letting out on Lois the pent-up anger she felt toward Daniel.

Lois glared at her in response. "Emily, I'm doing everything I can. I don't have time to be a babysitter as well."

Emily was shocked to hear Lois answer back. But it was a wake-up call, and one she needed. She'd put her staff under a lot of undue stress recently, first with the long honeymoon, then with the last-minute vacation to England. Lois, of all her staff, had been at the front and center of it all. Serena had barely been working at the inn.

"You're right, I'm sorry," Emily said. But her mind was on Chantelle now. She didn't want her left alone, especially not while her behavior was still wobbly. "Lois, let's have a meeting later. Talk about a raise."

Lois looked stunned as Emily walked away. She was usually so timid, Emily thought, she must have shocked herself. Tension was certainly running high at the moment. The whole inn seemed to be saturated with stress.

She walked through the corridors and out into the conservatory. But Chantelle wasn't there.

A sensation of panic took hold of Emily almost immediately.

"Chantelle?" she called, glancing around her. "Chantelle, where are you?"

Through the glass windows she caught sight of the outbuilding, the one where the spa was being constructed, the one where the unused swimming pool was. There was no one onsite. What if she'd wandered in and hurt herself?

Emily raced out of the conservatory and across the gardens, heading for the outhouse, calling Chantelle's name loudly. Some of the guests who were out enjoying the lawns looked at her with concerned expressions.

"Have you seen my daughter?" she asked them frantically.

They shook their heads and she hurried on, into the building site of the outhouse.

"Chantelle?" she shouted, her voice echoing through the vast, empty space. "Are you there?"

But the girl didn't respond. Emily felt her panic intensifying.

As she looked frantically about her, she felt an old familiar sensation, one she hadn't had for a while. She was slipping back into her memories.

"Not now," she muttered, lowering to the floor as blackness overtook her vision.

Suddenly, Charlotte materialized before her eyes. Not healthy happy Charlotte, but the cold, limp dead version lying floppy and still in her father's arms. Emily watched, stunned, unable to speak, unable to comprehend what was happening. Charlotte was so pale but it looked just like she was sleeping.

Roy looked up at her, pain etched into every pore on his face. "It's okay, sweetie," he said. "Charlotte's hurt, that's all. I'll make her better. You don't need to be scared."

A hand clasped down on Emily's shoulder and she screamed. Turning sharply, she saw that it was Chantelle standing beside her. Not Charlotte. Not a ghost. She was back to the present day.

"Mommy? What are you doing?" Chantelle asked, looking terrified at the sight of Emily on her knees.

Sobs racked through Emily's body. She heaved Chantelle into her arms, holding her tightly, and wept.

*

Daniel missed dinner that evening, leaving Emily and Chantelle to eat alone. Chantelle seemed weary of Emily after the episode in the outhouse, and Emily felt ashamed of her behavior. Her own father had managed to keep his composure and try to alleviate her worry while his dead daughter lay in his arms, but Emily herself wasn't able to reassure Chantelle in the same way. She felt like a failure.

After eating, they retired to the living room. Chantelle got on with the clock tinkering she'd continued practicing since their return from England, while Emily stared absent-mindedly at the unlit fireplace. Mogsy lay curled on the couch beside her, and she stroked one of her long ears for comfort.

There was a knock on the door. Emily turned, frowning. It wasn't often they were disturbed in the living room. The door opened and Marnie looked around, her face flustered.

"Let me guess," Emily said. "Professor Vaughn has a problem?"

Marnie chewed her lip and nodded. "He's in the dining room," she said. "Demanding to see the manager."

Emily sighed and stood, patting Mogsy as she looked up at her and whined.

Emily followed Marnie into the dining room. Inside she saw the same handful of guests from the other night trying their best to avoid Professor Vaughn's disturbance. Matthew was standing beside the professor looking upset, trying his best to calm him down.

"What's the matter here?" Emily asked, sounding weary.

"I was just telling your chef that his steak has been overcooked. It has the consistency of rubber."

Matthew looked at her, his eyes pained. "This is the third one he's tried to send back. He said the first one was overcooked, the second raw, now overcooked again."

"Then your silly little waitress," Professor Vaughn continued ranting, "refused to take this one back to the kitchen!"

Emily gritted her teeth. She'd just about had enough of this. The atmosphere in the room was toxic. It was like Professor Vaughn had the blackest aura in the world, and everyone who came into contact with him became contaminated with his gloom.

"I think it would be best for you to check out now," Emily stated.

She could practically feel everyone in the room hold their breath with shock.

"What?" Professor Vaughn barked.

Emily folded her arms. "I won't tolerate your attitude anymore," she told him. "You have my staff running around after you, changing your towels, recooking your dinner. We've done all we can to satisfy your demands and I think it would be best for everyone if we accepted that that cannot be achieved. I would like you to check out now. I will give you a full refund."

Out the corner of her eye she caught sight of Matthew and Marnie smiling victoriously. It must be vindicating for them to have Emily stand up for them like this. But Emily herself didn't feel like a winner. Losing the carriage house income didn't exactly thrill her. But her other guests were her priority and Professor Vaughn was clearly ruining their stay. Not to mention her staff. They shouldn't have to put up with that kind of treatment.

Professor Vaughn stood, his face red with rage. "How dare you!" he yelled, throwing his napkin onto the table. "As if I'd want to stay another night in a horrific place like this!"

He stormed out of the dining room.

Emily's whole body felt like an elastic band about to snap. But suddenly she heard clapping coming from behind her. She looked around. The other diners were applauding.

She laughed. Marnie and Matthew came over and hugged her.

"Thank you," Marnie said, clearly understanding the financial sacrifice Emily had just made for their behalf.

It buoyed Emily to see her guests and staff supporting her.

"Can you get everyone a free glass of wine," she said to Marnie.

"You bet," the girl replied, grinning, with a renewed spring in her step.

Emily left the dining room and watched from the door of the inn as Professor Vaughn threw his suitcase into the back of his car and sped off. Any other day, she'd have felt good about having stood up for herself, her staff, and her guests. But instead, she felt hollowed out, in need of support.

Emily was in desperate need of a friend. She'd call Amy but was always offloading on her. She knew Jayne would be hopeless and unhelpful. There was Yvonne but she felt like she'd been relying on her generosity too much recently, and Suzanna was busy with baby Robin. Serena seemed more distant than ever.

She checked her watch. It would be afternoon in England. Maybe she could call her father. But he had so much on his plate right now, the last thing she wanted to do was add to his worries. She didn't want to burden him with her emotions.

That only left one person. It was time, Emily realized.

She scrolled through her contacts and stopped at Patricia's number. Then she hit dial.

Patricia answered in her typically dry way, as if the sight of her only living daughter calling her roused no emotion in her whatsoever.

"I wondered when I'd hear from you," she said.

"You can always call me, Mom," Emily reminded her.

Already their call had gotten off on the wrong foot.

"Mom, I don't want to bicker," Emily said. "Please. I have some news."

"You're pregnant," Patricia replied.

Emily faltered. Had she guessed or had someone told her? Jayne could be a blabbermouth but surely she hadn't let that slip.

"Yes," Emily replied, sounding a little shell-shocked. "How did you know?"

"It's inevitable," Patricia replied. "I'm just glad you waited until you were married. So, when's it due?"

Her mom's tone riled Emily. She sounded so unenthusiastic, and referring to the baby as *it* felt even worse.

"Early December," she told her.

"Great," Patricia scoffed. "More gifts to get during the holiday period."

Her words stung Emily. "Is that all you have to say?" she challenged her mom. "No congratulations? Aren't you excited to become a grandmother?"

"Yes, yes," Patricia replied impatiently. "Congratulations. The miracle of life. All that. So it's healthy? You've had all your tests? You do know older mothers are more susceptible to babies with genetic abnormalities, don't you? I did tell you to have them sooner but you insisted on leaving it."

It was literally the last thing Emily wanted to hear from her mom. She was already stressing about the blood test results. Speaking to her mom had just worried her more.

She ended the call, feeling on the verge of breaking down. Just then, Daniel came in. He looked exhausted as he sat on the couch next to her, tipping his head back and closing his eyes.

"What a day…" he muttered.

"I just told my mom about the baby," Emily told him. She tucked her feet beneath her, wanting to become as small as possible.

Daniel opened his weary eyes and peered at her. "It didn't go well, I take it."

Emily shook her head, and now her tears came. She felt arms wrap around her, Daniel from the side and Chantelle from behind. Their comfort made her cry even more.

"It's okay, Mommy," Chantelle said soothingly.

"Thank you, sweetie."

"Come on," Daniel said. "Let's head up to bed. Mommy needs some rest."

They all went upstairs, Emily still weeping profusely. Chantelle hugged her tightly before retiring to her room. Daniel led her into the master bedroom and sat her onto the bed. He sat beside her.

"What's wrong, sweetheart?" he asked tenderly.

"What's right?" Emily wept bitterly into her hands. "My mom can't even pretend to be happy for me. Chantelle's still acting out. She wandered off today and I couldn't find her. I was so stressed I had a flashback, the most horrible one, of when Dad was trying to revive Charlotte." She gazed up at Daniel, her features etched with pain. "And Dad… Dad…" She couldn't speak anymore.

"Emily…" Daniel said softly, encouraging her on.

"He's dying, Daniel," she told him. "He has cancer. A year at the most to live."

Daniel's features fell, his expression turning from tired and exhausted to devastated.

"When did you find out?" he asked.

"In England, just before we left."

"Why didn't you tell me?"

Emily frowned at him. Was that all he had to say on the matter? "I didn't want to ruin your holiday. And I'd only just found out myself. I was still processing it."

Daniel ran his hands through his hair. He looked like he was despairing. "That's not the sort of thing you should keep to yourself," he stammered. "We're a team, Emily. We're supposed to do things together, tell each other everything."

"We're a team?" she snapped. "Since when? All you ever want to do is fix up the house!"

Daniel's face snapped toward her, his features now showing fury. "For you. For us. For our family. You make it sound like I'm doing it to avoid you or something!"

"Sometimes it feels like you are," Emily replied. She knew she was lashing out, but her emotions had gotten the better of her. "Sometimes it feels like you don't even want this baby at all."

"How can you say that?" Daniel exclaimed, exasperated.

"You don't do anything to show you're excited! You were nice when I was sick at first but now you're just bored of comforting me." Emily could hear her own paranoid accusations and cringed. Her hormones must be playing some part in this sudden outpouring of anger and rage.

"That's unfair," Daniel told her.

She glared at him. "Is it? Then look me in the eye and tell me you're excited about the baby. That it's your dream come true like it is mine."

"I'm not playing your games," Daniel said, standing, shaking with rage.

He stormed out of the room.

Emily stared at his retreating figure, mouth agape.

He had given her nothing, not even an unsatisfactory answer, just silence.

And it only made her feel worse.

CHAPTER TWENTY FOUR

When Emily awoke the next day, Daniel had already left for work. She sighed, disappointed.

Checking her phone, she saw she'd received a text late last night from Amy. She'd organized a surprise baby shower for midday that day. It was the last thing that Emily felt like doing.

She got out of bed and went to wake Chantelle, then the two of them headed downstairs for breakfast. For the first time in a long time, the inn was quiet.

"Amy's planned a surprise party for me today," Emily told Chantelle as she made her cereal. She came over and put it on the table.

"Why?" Chantelle asked. "It's not your birthday, is it?"

Emily shook her head. "It's called a baby shower. When a woman is pregnant her friends and family throw a party with food and games and gifts for the baby."

Chantelle looked disgusted by the prospect. "So the baby gets a party before it's even born?" she stated, looking unimpressed.

Emily felt her mood sink even further. Chantelle's jealousy was not something she had the reserves to deal with right now.

"Should I take that to mean you don't want to come?" Emily asked.

Chantelle folded her arms. "I don't want to come."

"But you love a party."

Chantelle looked away, busying herself with her cereal.

"Fine," Emily muttered. She'd have to organize a sitter. But surely all her friends would be at the party? Who'd be available to look after Chantelle? Leaving her with Lois was definitely off the cards.

She texted Amy. *Bit of a problem. Chantelle doesn't want to come. She's jealous of the baby. But I don't know who is available to look after her.*

Amy's reply came quickly after. *Don't worry. I'll think of something.*

Emily put her phone away and ate her plain toast. She skipped out on a warm drink this morning, instead having water, wanting her breakfast to be as bland as possible as per Doctor Arkwright's advice.

Emily's phone buzzed with an incoming text. It was from Amy.

Okay, Chantelle is taken care of. There'll be someone round to collect her in an hour.

How mysterious, Emily thought. She wondered what Amy had planned.

Thirty minutes later, the doorbell rang and Emily got up to answer it. To her surprise, a lady was standing there in a full-blown princess outfit, looking like she'd stepped off the pages of a fantasy story.

"Hi, I'm Princess Esmeralda Featherton," she announced. "I'm here to take Chantelle Morey on her magical adventure day."

Emily's eyes widened. "Um… did Amy book you?"

The lady smiled and dropped the princess act. "Yeah, I'm mainly a party entertainer but I also do adventure days out. It's usually for sick kids and stressed parents. Which one are you?"

Emily pointed at the dark bags under her eyes. "Can't you guess?"

She laughed. Trust Amy to come up with such a creative solution to the problem!

"So what magical things do you have planned for Chantelle then?" Emily asked.

"Well, we'll take the magic pumpkin down to the beach," Princess Esmeralda began, jerking her thumb behind her to where Emily saw, with surprise, a Cinderella carriage attached to the back of two white horses. "There's a picnic table there with tea, sandwiches, and cakes. We'll have a little tea party, get our nails painted and our hair done. Sound good?"

"It sounds marvelous," Emily replied. She turned and called over her shoulder. "Hey, Chantelle, I think there's someone here to see you."

The woman transformed her expression back into the airy-fairy princess one she'd had when Emily first answered the door. Chantelle appeared at the end of the corridor, looking suspicious. She walked slowly toward them. With each step, her face seemed to light up more and more.

"I'm Princess Esmeralda Featherton," the lady said, curtseying. "You must be Princess Chantelle." She gestured behind her. "Your carriage awaits."

Chantelle's eyes bulged at the sight of the pumpkin and horses. She looked up at Emily, shocked. "Is this for me?"

Emily nodded, amused by the whole charade, and encouraged Chantelle out the door.

"I'll drop her back in the afternoon," Princess Esmeralda said with a wink. Then to Chantelle, she added, "Your cape, gloves, and crown are in the carriage. Hurry, we can't be late for our tea party."

Emily laughed as she watched Chantelle hop into the carriage. Then off they went, the horses clip-clopping down the driveway. It was the strangest sight she'd ever seen.

She texted Amy. *You're crazy. But also a genius.*

Then she headed off to her baby shower, in better spirits than she'd felt in days.

*

Emily drove to Karen's bakery where the baby shower was to be held. When she walked in, she was surprised to see the whole place had been decorated in beautiful white and pink ribbons. Karen had laid out the entire table with cakes and sandwiches, though Emily wasn't sure whether her delicate stomach would be able to handle any of them.

Sitting around the table, smiling at her brightly, were Yvonne, Amy, Suzanna—who seemed to already have miraculously returned to her pre-pregnancy shape—Sunita, and, of course, Karen.

"Guys," Emily said, breathlessly, shocked and elated by the effort they'd put in for her.

"Sit down, sit down," Karen instructed her.

Emily's friends took it in turn to hand her gifts. She opened them each. A bottle sterilizer from Yvonne. A set of baby onesies from Karen. Sunita had gifted her a beautiful nightlight that played white noise and projected images of stars onto the ceiling. She received a bathtub donut in the shape of a sunflower from Suzanna, and finally, from Amy, a voucher for a ridiculously expensive-looking baby photographer in Maine.

"This is so wonderful," Emily said, overwhelmed by their gratitude.

They jumped into the food and drinks, and Amy quizzed Emily over how everything was going with the pregnancy.

"It's not too bad," Emily said. "The nausea is the worst. And all the tests are making me anxious."

"What kind of tests?" Amy asked.

"Well, the other day I had to have four vials of blood taken," Emily said, showing her the small bruise still visible in the crook of her elbow. "It's the genetic abnormalities test." The moment the words were out of her mouth, she remembered her mother's voice, remembered the anxiety it had further instilled in her. And she remembered the way Daniel had seemed entirely uninterested.

"Em…" Amy said, touching her hand gently. "What's wrong?"

Before she even had time to think, Emily burst into tears. She dropped her head into her arms on the table.

"Babe, you can talk to me," Amy assured her, her arm slung around Emily's shoulder. "I'm here for you."

But it was too much. Emily couldn't speak about her fears. She stood. "I'm sorry, I have to go now," she said.

Amy stood too. "Em, don't go like this."

Everyone looked at Emily with expressions of concern. Embarrassed, Emily hurried out of the store. She walked quickly to her car and got inside, breathing deeply, feeling panicked. She desperately wanted to speak to her dad. It would be seven a.m. in England. He'd have been up and awake since five, watering the garden, so she dialed his new number.

He answered the call after several minutes of ringing.

"Sorry, darling, I couldn't find the right button to push. How are you?"

"Dad…" Emily whimpered, then she broke down again in sobs.

"Oh, darling," Roy replied. His voice was calmer and kinder than ever. "Tell me what's wrong."

Emily hadn't wanted to burden him, especially with what he was going through, but she needed him right now. Him and only him. Her father could console her in ways Patricia never could, or Daniel or Amy for that matter. Roy alone had a unique ability to put her fears to rest. How was she going to cope when he was gone?

"It's everything," she stammered. "I'm worried about the baby, and having to have so many tests doesn't help with my anxiety. Daniel is so focused on work it's like he's not even here. I can't even tell if he wants the baby. We had a huge fight last night. It was horrible. I'm trying to slow down and reduce my stress but the inn seems to fall apart whenever I'm not there to keep an eye on it. Lois has been great but I need someone to replace Serena because she's never available. I think she's mad at me after Chantelle's meltdown but she's never around to talk it through. And Chantelle is just a nightmare at the moment. I know you think she's the sweetest kid in the world, and she mostly is, but God can that girl tantrum."

Emily spoke quickly, all her words tumbling out of her, all her fears spilling as quickly as her tears. Roy listened patiently, just as she'd needed someone to do all along.

"And, Dad, you're going to leave me!" she wailed. "Again! I thought I was going to be okay but now I feel terrified about it. I had a flashback, to Charlotte after she'd died." She stumbled over the words. She and her father didn't talk that openly or often about Charlotte's death. "I remembered you telling me it was okay. She was dead and you knew nothing was going to bring her back but somehow you still had the strength to comfort me, to put me first. I don't know how you did it. How am I going to cope without you?"

Once she was done offloading, he finally spoke.

"Emily Jane, you are a strong woman," he began. "I couldn't be prouder of you."

"I don't feel very strong right now, crying in my car!"

"Who ever told you crying is a sign of weakness?" Roy challenged her. "Expressing your feelings is the most important thing you can do for your health. That's how I was able to do it, to always put you first, by shutting my emotions down. I'd always been taught not to feel, young men of my generation were. And what happened? I snapped. But not you, Emily Jane. You are strong enough to feel, to let yourself experience pain."

"If it's so good, why does it feel so crappy?" Emily said, weeping bitterly.

She heard Roy chuckle kind-heartedly over the phone. "Oh, my darling, I wish you could see yourself through my eyes. You're remarkable. You already have the solution to your problem, you just need someone to reassure you it's the right thing to do."

"What solution?" Emily asked.

"Communication," Roy replied. "You know you need to speak to Daniel about his behavior and feelings but you're scared to do it because of a deep held insecurity that he wants to leave. An insecurity my leaving instilled in you."

"No, Dad, don't start this again. I've forgiven you, completely. I don't want you to feel guilty about anything that happened in the past anymore."

"I know," he said. "And your ability to forgive is another thing that's so remarkable about you. But I am not saying this for me, but for you, my treasure. You know that you avoid speaking to Daniel because you're worried he'll confirm whatever paranoia you have. But I think another part of you knows that he is committed to you, he loves you. You're married, you're a team. He's not going anywhere."

Emily listened, comforted by her father's words. "You sound like a therapist," she said.

"I've had many years of counseling," he quipped. "And I also have life experience. Marriage is hard. Having kids is hard. There is a constant flux, an ebb and flow. But if you don't communicate continually things won't fix themselves. I regret all those times I shut Patricia out, shouted her down. I know you and your mother struggle to get along, but Emily Jane, *I* was the reason our marriage failed, *I'm* the reason she is the way she is."

"Dad..." Emily warned.

"I'm not being self-pitying," he interjected. "I'm speaking facts. If I'd been a better man, if I'd spoken and communicated and felt and cried when I needed to, things would have been completely different. You and Daniel aren't like Patricia and I. You can do those things. You can work things out."

Emily took a deep breath, bolstered by her father's encouragement. Having him in her life at the moment was the most wonderful thing. Imagining him no longer being there was an agony she didn't want to have to go through.

"Now, are you writing me letters?" Roy asked. "Because I've already written ten for you."

"Ten?" Emily exclaimed. "But I haven't received anything."

"Oh, I'm not going to mail these," Roy said. "These are my memories of you. A letter per photograph, written like a diary entry. I want to record everything I can remember about you, right down to what you ate, what you wore, how I felt as I held you in my arms."

"Really?" Emily asked, overwhelmed at the thought. "You're doing that for me?"

"Yes," Roy said. "It's my big project. And I only have a year to get it done."

Emily felt beyond touched that her father had decided to spend his final months on earth creating such a wonderful gift for her.

"I love you, Dad," she said. "Thank you for everything."

"I love you too, sweetheart."

They ended the call. Emily felt much better.

She was finally ready to have the talk with Daniel.

*

Daniel came home very late again that evening, when Emily was already in bed. But she wasn't sleeping, just resting, and she turned to him as he tiptoed into the room.

"Sorry, did I wake you?" he whispered.

"I wasn't sleeping," Emily replied. She sat up, propping some pillows behind her back so she was comfortable. "I was waiting for you to come back so we could talk about last night."

"Oh," Daniel said.

Emily watched his silhouette moving around the room, removing his clothing. He approached her and slid into bed.

"Do you mean talk or are you just going to shout at me again?" he asked.

"I mean talk," Emily said, reaching out and touching his chest. She'd read somewhere that maintaining physical contact with your spouse during arguments was a good way to stay connected, because it reduced the distance and reminded you of how close you really were.

"I'm really tired," Daniel sighed. "Can't we talk tomorrow?"

Emily shook her head. "Nope. It has to be tonight. Tomorrow you'll be working again, and you'll be tired again, and nothing will have been resolved."

He sighed. "Fine. What do you want to talk about?"

Emily kept her voice calm and firm. "I want to understand what you're feeling about the baby and the pregnancy. There's been some distance between us recently and I don't know why. I keep worrying that it's because of the baby, because you don't really want her."

Daniel shook his head. "I really hate you saying that," he said. "I want the baby, I do. I'm just, I don't know, scared. Chantelle shook everything up with us, what if Charlotte does too, once she's here? I almost lost you before and I'm scared that will happen again."

"Things will change, of course," Emily said. "But we'll work through our difficulties. We always do."

He nodded. "I'm just feeling a lot of pressure right now. I want to be able to provide for the whole family but I don't know if I can. You're working so hard and I just want to make things easier for you by getting the renovation done as quickly as possible. I want you to put your feet up for as much of this pregnancy as possible. And then when Charlotte's born, I don't want you to think you have to go back to work right away. I want you to have the option to spend time with her, because quite frankly I want to spend time with her too, since I missed out on the first six years with Chantelle. There's just so much going on in my head, Emily. Like, can I be a good dad? What about Chantelle? Will she feel left out?"

Emily listened patiently, just as her father had done with her. It turned out that Daniel shared many of the same anxieties as she did.

"Do you feel better for having gotten that all off your chest?" Emily asked him when he was finished.

"Yeah, actually." He turned and took her hands. "I'm sorry if I've been a jerk. I just didn't know how to deal with everything."

"Communication," Emily said. "For both of us."

Daniel nodded in agreement. "I promise I'll talk about my feelings more from now on, okay?"

Just then, there was a knock on the door. Emily frowned. It was very late and the staff wouldn't usually disturb her in the night. She got up and unlocked the door. Chantelle was standing there.

"Are you okay, honey?" Emily asked. "Can't you sleep?"

Chantelle rubbed her eyes. Emily let her into the master bedroom and she got up onto the bed, snuggling beside her father. Emily climbed in the other side.

"Daddy was just telling me about how he's a bit scared about when the baby comes," Emily told her.

Chantelle looked surprised. "Daddy doesn't get scared," she said.

"I do sometimes," Daniel told her. "About things that really matter. Like how you're feeling about having a sister."

Chantelle looked down, as though ashamed. "I don't want you to love her more than me," she said.

Emily and Daniel both hugged Chantelle tightly.

"We'll love you both the same," Emily said. "Just like how I love Daddy the same as I love you. And how I love Papa Roy just as much."

"So there won't be less love to share?" Chantelle asked.

Daniel answered this time. "Nope. There'll be more. The more people you love in life the more love you feel. It's the only thing in math that makes no sense."

Chantelle giggled. She was a math whiz so the analogy sat well with her. "So love is multiplied," she said. "Not subtracted."

"Exactly," Emily agreed.

Chantelle seemed very satisfied with the explanation. They snuggled together in bed. Emily was relieved they'd all finally had the chance to hash out their feelings. She could tell by the way both Chantelle and Daniel fell asleep so quickly that their minds were also unburdened and at ease.

For the first time in a long time, Emily felt as if the tide was turning for the better.

CHAPTER TWENTY FIVE

Emily felt significantly better the next morning, waking beside Chantelle and Daniel. They went down to breakfast happy and smiling.

Emily went to collect the mail and returned with a thank-you letter from the bride whose wedding had been saved by Roman's guest appearance and the last-minute catering skills of her friends. She folded it back up, satisfied.

They cooked a hearty breakfast and had just sat down to eat when Daniel received a call. He looked up at Emily as his phone continued ringing.

"This is work. Okay if I take it?" he asked.

Emily nodded in agreement and Daniel excused himself to take the call. When he came back, he was grinning.

"I've hired new contractors to replace the firm who didn't show up," he said. "They were just confirming to accept the job. Hopefully everything will get back on track at Trevor's now, and I'll be able to get back to doing up the spa."

"Yay!" Chantelle cried, punching the air.

Things seemed to be looking up, at last, Emily thought.

Just then, Chantelle's eyes widened with surprise. "I've worked out the clue!"

Emily looked at her curiously. "What clue?"

"From Charlotte's time capsule," Chantelle said. "I thought she meant it was somewhere on the beach or on an island nearby, but maybe she meant that it was buried in the outhouse, in the old swimming pool."

Emily considered what Chantelle was saying. The renovation work had taken place during their childhoods, so it was conceivable that Charlotte would have been able to hide the second time capsule in the cement before it dried over.

"I think you might be right!" Emily exclaimed.

They all stood and hurried to the outhouse. Much of the cement flooring had already been dug up, though Daniel had had to abandon work there to take over at Trevor's. His tools still lay strewn around the place.

"If she said you'd have to swim, then it will be this end, right?" Chantelle said, pointing to the furthest part from the door.

Daniel grabbed his pickaxe and hard hat then hurried over and started cleaving out the ground. The cement came out in chunks, in big slabs.

"Let me have a turn!" Emily said.

It looked very therapeutic. Digging up the old, the bad memories, ready to replace them with something new entirely.

"Are you sure, pregnant lady?" Daniel asked.

Emily nodded. Daniel transferred the hard hat from his own head to Emily's. Then she took the pickaxe in her hands and brought it down hard against the floor. She felt a satisfying crack as the ground disintegrated in the spot she'd hit.

"Oh, that felt good." She grinned.

"Can I do it?" Chantelle asked, excited.

Daniel put the hard hat on her next and Emily handed her the pickaxe. Chantelle wobbled a little under the weight of it, but managed to beat it down on the cement and cause a shard to separate from the main part.

"Look!" Emily cried, seeing that Chantelle's blast had exposed a foreign object in the cement.

"A tin." Chantelle beamed.

Daniel took over with the final work, releasing the tin finally. He handed it to Emily.

This time as she took it in her hands, she didn't feel surprised or shocked or grief-stricken. She felt happy, as though Charlotte had somehow known to bury her time capsules so that Emily could one day find them and draw comfort from them.

They took the time capsule onto the porch and opened it up. The first thing Emily saw lying on the top was a toy telescope, one they'd played with as children. Then she fished out a necklace that had all the trademark signs of having been made by Roy. She handed it to Chantelle.

"What do you think—a Papa Roy original?"

Chantelle clutched it in her hand. "Oh yes, definitely. Can I wear it?"

"Of course," Emily said.

She helped affix it around the child's neck as Chantelle continued rummaging in the tin.

"Look, Mommy," she said, holding up a small pink, woolen hat. It wasn't a child's hat, nor a doll's. It was a hat for a newborn baby.

A jolt struck Emily's heart. It was as if Charlotte had known that one day she would be having a baby girl in the winter. The thought of putting this little woolen hat on newborn Baby Charlotte's head filled her to the brim with emotion.

They spent the afternoon looking through all the wonderful things inside the box. Of course, Charlotte hadn't stopped at two. There was another clue for another time capsule. Emily smiled to herself, treasuring it, looking forward to the time when it too could be unearthed. What other premonitions had Charlotte made about Emily's future and life? What other signs had she left for her sister to find all these years later? The thought no longer spooked her, but comforted her.

Because Emily was absolutely certain that Charlotte was with her, smiling at her, encouraging her to live her life to the fullest.

And she just couldn't wait for the next sign.

*

The time came for Emily to collect her blood test results from Doctor Arkwright. She and Daniel discussed him attending, but decided in the end that it would be better for him to continue working on the spa. Emily was glad they were able to have an actual conversation about it and come to an agreement. It was what she'd wanted all along.

Doctor Arkwright welcomed Emily into her office.

"It's all good news," she said. "The tests are fine. There's nothing to worry about."

Emily let out a sigh of relief.

"I'm glad you came alone, actually," Doctor Arkwright said. "I noticed you and your husband were in a tense place last time. I wanted to find out how your stress levels have been."

Emily smiled. "There was a rocky patch but we've worked through it now."

"I'm glad to hear that. And your job? You said it was very busy at the moment."

"I'm going to hire some more staff," Emily said. She'd decided it was worth the extra expense if it meant more time to relax and take care of herself. Lois, too, needed some more help around the place. She'd been working like a trouper; it was only fair.

"Wonderful news. Well, in that case, I won't need to see you again for four weeks." She checked her schedule. "Ah, that falls on Labor Day weekend, so we'll meet up a little after that." She booked something in and handed Emily the appointment slip. "Do you have anything fun planned for the long weekend?" she asked.

"I do," Emily said. "My friend is playing a concert in Portland. He's a local musician and is launching his new album that weekend."

The doctor raised her eyebrows. "That sounds exciting indeed." Then a flicker crossed her eyes. They widened. "This is probably a silly stab in the dark, but it's not Roman Westbrook by any chance, is it? I read he moved to Maine recently and his album is being released on Labor Day."

Emily laughed. "Yes, it is."

The usually composed and professional Doctor Arkwright looked completely stunned, like she'd seen a ghost. "I'm a huge fan," she spluttered.

It amused Emily to see her turn into a giggling fangirl. To think she'd ever found Doctor Arkwright imposing!

"I'll see if I can get a copy of his album for you," Emily said. "For our next appointment. I'm sure he won't mind signing it."

"Thank you!" Doctor Arkwright exclaimed.

Emily left the office and returned home. When she got there, Daniel was already sitting on the porch reading a book with Chantelle. They'd made a picnic and laid it out on the table.

"What's all this?" Emily asked, smiling as she drew closer.

"The new contractors are amazing," Daniel explained. "They're a new, local company, run by a couple of fresh college graduates. They're so efficient I didn't need to supervise them at all today, so the work I wanted to get done in the spa today is done. I thought we could spend a relaxing evening together."

Emily was so touched. Daniel had really taken their conversation to heart and she could tell he was going out of his way to make it up to her. Chantelle, too, seemed to have returned to her usual sweet self.

Emily came and sat with them. She noticed as she did that all the foods were completely plain. Plain rice. Plain bread. Plain chips. Plain fries. And of course, a large jug of water, non-sparkling, and not a drop of juice in sight. She laughed, delighted.

"This is so sweet!"

"That's Chantelle's special non-alcoholic cocktail recipe," Daniel said, pouring her a glass of water, which he topped with a mini umbrella.

"It's two parts water with an equal amount of water, but a splash of water at the end," Chantelle said. "Stirred, of course. Not shaken."

Emily dissolved into giggles.

Daniel dished her out a portion of the blandest foods and she began devouring it happily.

"So how were the test results?" Daniel asked.

"It's all good," she said. "Doctor Arkwright was really happy. My blood pressure is fine now as well."

"That's great news," Daniel said.

"Are you ready for dessert?" Chantelle asked.

Emily hadn't been able to tolerate anything sugary so couldn't begin to imagine what could substitute as a bland dessert.

"Sure…" she said curiously.

Chantelle grinned and ran inside. When she came back, she was carrying a plate. On it was a single rice cake, which she'd cut in quarters.

"Cake!" she exclaimed, giggling.

Emily took her piece, thoroughly amused and touched by the whole evening. Then she kicked back and smiled, breathing in the ocean air. The end of summer was already in sight, and she could hardly believe it.

But she felt, overwhelmingly, that everything was going to be OK after all.

CHAPTER TWENTY SIX

4 WEEKS LATER

Emily dove into a breakfast of eggs, toast, and bacon, with ketchup on the side and garlic fried mushrooms. Her morning sickness had finally passed, and she was making up for lost time by eating everything Baby Charlotte demanded.

Her bump was visible now, and she'd had to invest in a maternity wardrobe. She'd stocked up on floral maxi dresses for the last days of summer, and warmer cotton ones for when fall arrived.

"I'm so excited for Roman's concert tonight," Chantelle said.

"Me too," Emily replied. "A limo journey to Portland sounds like just the kind of relaxing way to spend my time that Doctor Arkwright ordered."

"First," Daniel said, "we've got the beach celebrations for Labor Day. We're meeting Amy and Harry down there."

"Yay!" Chantelle exclaimed. "Will it be just as fun as the Fourth of July was?"

"I'm sure it will," Emily told her.

They finished eating and headed down to the beach, strolling very slowly as Emily now did.

Amy and Harry were already there, along with lots of other Sunset Harbor residents. Chantelle ran off with her friends to play in the water. Daniel and Emily sat down opposite the happy couple on one of the picnic benches.

"So what is your plan?" Emily asked Amy. "Now that summer is over? Are you going back to New York City?"

Amy looked at Harry. "We thought maybe I could stay a little longer."

Emily was surprised to hear it.

"I mean, it worked out so well for you," Amy added, and she eyed Emily's wedding ring subtly as she spoke.

Emily knew exactly what Amy was trying to tell her. Harry was the One. Her summer in Sunset Harbor had confirmed it. She wanted the ring.

A spark of excitement set Emily alight. Could Amy really be considering settling down? She stood suddenly. Daniel looked up at her and frowned.

"You okay?"

"Yes," Emily said hurriedly. "I just remembered that I wanted to show Amy something. On the beach." She searched her mind for an excuse. "A washed up jellyfish."

Daniel looked perturbed. Amy was practically wincing from how obvious Emily's lie was. Even Harry seemed to have worked out that Emily was just trying to get her friend away from the men for a romance conversation. He smiled faintly and shook his head.

"We won't be long," Amy said, standing and grasping Emily's arm. "What was that?" she hissed as they walked away across the sand. "A jellyfish?"

"I'm sorry, I have baby brain fog," Emily said. "But never mind that. We got away so now we can talk privately. I caught the way you looked at my ring. Are you and Harry thinking about marrying?"

Amy was silent for a moment, and Emily wondered if the question had stirred up painful memories for her friend, of Fraser, of how badly it ended with him, how her fairytale ending had been dashed once before.

"If everything stayed like this forever," Amy said, "I'd marry him tomorrow. A million percent."

Emily wanted to scream with delight. The thought of Amy moving to Sunset Harbor filled her with happiness. But her friend was holding something back.

"But what's the problem?" Emily asked.

Amy sighed. "The fact that things do change," she said, a little sadly. "What if the very reason it works so well is the fact I have another life in New York City I can return to at any time? Maybe the fact I'm independent—financially and in terms of assets—is what makes it so wonderful. If I joined all that stuff with Harry, had a house, a kid, a cat, how will I know that it won't drive me crazy?"

"I guess you just have to take a leap of faith sometimes, Ames," Emily said. "You can't plan everything, especially not the future. So sometimes you just close your eyes, cross your fingers, and jump."

Amy looked tenderly at her friend and smiled. "It sounds so easy when you say it like that."

Emily shrugged. "Because sometimes it is. Sometimes it just works. I don't know why, the timing, the motivation, the stage of your life, the compatibility of your partner. Sometimes it just works out fine." She squeezed Amy's arm where it was looped with hers. "Remember when you started the business? It was a whim. And it's brought you nothing but success and happiness. It's opened a million doors for you, not to mention paid for a thousand pairs of shoes I'm jealous of." Amy laughed. Emily carried on. "Back then you were young and you didn't overthink things. You just jumped into it, feet first. Maybe Harry is another thing you need to jump into feet first."

"That sounds painful," Amy quipped. Then she turned a little serious. "Okay, I'm glad you said all that. I thought maybe you'd tell me not to rush again because of what happened with Fraser. It's good to know you've got my back."

Emily noticed the twinkle in Amy's eye. She narrowed her own, suspiciously.

"Have you already made a decision about this?" she guessed.

A grin burst across Amy's face. She nodded vigorously. "Yup. I'm moving to Sunset Harbor. Harry and I are buying a house together."

Emily couldn't believe it. She screamed loudly, then clapped a hand over her mouth as people turned to look at her.

"Amy!" she squealed, throwing her arms tightly around her friend's neck. "This is the best news I've had in ages!"

Her best friend was going to move here, was going to be available and accessible to her whenever she needed her. It felt like a dream come true, one Emily could hardly believe. But she couldn't be happier. Having her best friend closer would be the best thing in the world.

Everything was finally coming together.

*

After all the fun at the beach, they decided to take Chantelle out in the boat so she could see the rugged island they'd discovered on their romantic date earlier in the summer. As they strolled through town on the way to the harbor, Emily noticed how much quieter it was becoming. Once more, the town was emptying as summer came to a close. She had seen the inn through another successful summer and couldn't be more proud of herself and Daniel for getting through it all.

They climbed on board Daniel's boat and he sailed them through the ocean.

"Is this our last journey of the summer?" Chantelle asked sadly.

"It might be," Daniel said. "Unless we get some unseasonably warm weather in the fall. So you'd best savor it."

When they came ashore, Chantelle looked just as enamored with the island's natural, wild beauty as Daniel and Emily had been when they first set eyes on it.

"What would you do with an island like this if you owned it, Chantelle?" Daniel asked her as they strolled along hand in hand.

"I'd turn it into a magical land," Chantelle said. "A place to come for tea parties, like the one me and Princess Esmeralda had on the beach. There could be a boat like the Cinderella pumpkin that took you ashore, then a wooden palace in the treetops. It could have a ballroom for dancing in and a long table for the tea party."

Emily and Daniel exchanged a glance, amused by their daughter's imagination and creativity.

"That sounds like a lovely idea," Daniel said. "I wonder whether I'd have the woodworking skills to make a tree house that looked like a palace. And for a ballroom we could put in a dance floor and fill it with solar lamps, under a gazebo."

Just like the last time he'd been on the island, Emily saw that he was growing excited by the prospect of doing something there.

"I don't want to burst everyone's bubble," she said. "But remember we'd only be able to use the island if it were part of the inn. We can't afford just to own one if there isn't any money coming in."

"We're only imagining, Mommy," Chantelle said.

But Emily could tell Daniel was not. His mind was ticking overtime with thoughts. As Chantelle went to collect shells, she and Daniel sat together and discussed it some more.

"It could start as a fun boating destination for guests," Daniel said. "They could row here or take kayaks. Or maybe I could use my motorboat to shuffle some of our high-paying guests here. A perk."

"It's a cute idea," Emily said. "But what would they do while they were out here?"

"Well, we could hang some hammocks in the trees," Daniel suggested. "We could put in a fire pit for nighttime bonfires or for those who come over during colder weather."

"I still don't know who will want to spend any extended amount of time here, if there's no electricity."

"We can string solar lights," he said. "Bring lanterns and fuel. Not having electricity will be a selling point. Imagine how gorgeous the stars will look out here! People could come and meditate. Maybe Tracey could do one of her classes here. It would be the perfect retreat for a writer or artist or musician. Can you imagine? Someone who wants solitude, a quiet place away from the inn. I could build a cabin so people could stay for more time if they wanted to."

Emily loved his enthusiasm, but she still couldn't quite see it working. "But if there's no electricity, what happens in an emergency? Say your poor writer on their retreat gets stuck in a storm? Or they come down with appendicitis and need medical aid?"

"I'll drive over in the boat to get them. We could install a generator which has enough power at least for their cell phone. That way they can call the inn whenever they want, as well. Maybe I could drive them over supplies and things, or sail them back in order to dine at the inn."

"And what happens when they need to pee?"

Daniel laughed. "I'll build an outhouse."

Emily shook her head. "Kind of ruins the romance of it, don't you think?"

"It depends on how adventurous the guest is," Daniel said. He just wasn't letting this go, Emily realized. "Some people love to get a little bit back to nature."

"Without running water?" Emily added.

"We can dig a well!" came Daniel's response. "It is possible, you know, to dig your own pipes and wells and build plumbing. People did it themselves in the past!"

He seemed to have an answer for everything. Seeing how serious Daniel was, Emily started to actually consider his proposition. She thought about it from a marketing point of view, from the view of monetizing it.

"The Island Room," she said. "That sounds quite exotic and romantic, don't you think?"

Daniel nodded. "We could invite Colin Magnus out to try it and write an article. It would garner us lots of press. Even if we only have guests over the summer months each year it would pay for itself in a few years' time. And then it would generate enough money to pay for its upkeep, because really the maintenance would be minimal, once everything was up and running."

Emily thought even more deeply on the option. If all the work was upfront—building the tree house, the ballroom, the cabin, the outhouse, and a jetty for the boat—then after that it would be a case of maintaining it.

"Do you think your new contractors would be interested in taking on the work?" she asked.

"Absolutely," Daniel replied. "It would be amazing in their portfolio!"

Emily felt herself getting caught up in Daniel's enthusiasm. She began running the figures through in her mind, considering all the big families they'd had to turn away through lack of space.

"We could do with more big family units," she said. "So say we made it a two- or three-bed cabin. Then we'd be able to rent it out at a thousand dollars a night. One season of rentals would pay off the sale price. The next year the cost of renovating and building all the different places would be paid off. After two years, it's all profit. And we'd own it outright, so it's an asset we could sell later if the upkeep becomes too demanding."

"Exactly," Daniel said. "Although I'd love to hang onto it for the family. Even if we decide to not use it for the inn any longer in the future, we could still keep it as a family getaway for us and the girls. Whenever we want to, we can come out here and it will ground us, get us back to ground zero as a family, allowing some space from the inn. It would be fantastic for the kids. A childhood escape. Somewhere for them to really enjoy growing up."

Emily took Daniel's hands then. "Are we being crazy, or should we do this?" she asked.

Daniel shook his head. "It's not crazy at all. We've run through the figures. And if anyone can make it succeed, it's us."

Emily felt a swell of excitement at the prospect. She also felt proud of the achievements she and Daniel had made with the inn. They did make a great team, and together they were building something amazing for their family. Could they really do it?

Just then Chantelle skipped over. She was holding something in her hands. "Look what I found," she said, excitedly, holding out her hands.

Emily picked up the object resting in her palms. It was an old toy telescope, rusted, the glass cracked. A strange sense of familiarity hit Emily. She and Charlotte had a similar toy as a child. No, not similar, the exact same type! The same type they'd found in Charlotte's time capsule.

Chantelle gasped with disbelief, "It's just like Aunty Charlotte's!" she exclaimed, looking at it with awe.

With a growing sensation that this was some kind of sign, Emily turned the telescope over and saw there were faded letters etched into the side. She read them and gasped.

"Sunset Island," she said aloud.

The coincidence was too much. It was a sign, it had to be. The same toy she and Charlotte had played with as children washing up on an island she and Daniel were wondering about buying, with the name similar to her inn's on the side.

"Daniel," she gasped, clutching the telescope to her chest. "We should do it."

His eyes widened with excitement. "Really?"

"Yes." Emily nodded, more certain of this than anything. "Yes!"

"Do what?" Chantelle asked, confused, looking from her father to her mother with a frown.

"Buy an island," Daniel said, sounding like he couldn't believe his own words.

Chantelle laughed with disbelief. She clearly thought they were joking. "Only rich people can own islands," she said, dismissively, as though she were far too intelligent to fall for it.

"Not tiny islands like this one," Daniel told her. "There's no water, Wi-Fi, or electricity so the price is actually quite reasonable."

"Let's call the real estate agent to see if it's still for sale," Emily said. "The sign is so old and battered it may have been here for years for all we know. But if it's for sale, we will put an offer on it."

Chantelle was still frowning. She studied both of their faces. "Are you being serious?" she asked, her tone incredulous.

"Yes!" they both cried.

Chantelle sat there, frozen for a moment in disbelief. But the news must have finally sunk in because suddenly she was on her feet, hollering and whooping, charging around the rocky beach with her arms out wide.

"But," Daniel warned, once she returned, "we shouldn't get too ahead of ourselves. The island might not even still be for sale. Or the price might be different now and out of our range. It's still very much a tentative decision so don't get your hopes up too much."

Chantelle nodded, but clearly wasn't going to dampen her enthusiasm at all. The very idea her parents were going to *try* and buy an island seemed enough to delight her.

Emily and Daniel smiled at each other, excited for the future and what they hoped might be the beginning of a new adventure together.

*

They returned to the harbor to see that the Labor Day celebration at the yacht club was in full swing. A final horn sounded out for summer. But they couldn't join in the celebrations this year because they had Roman's album launch party to go to.

Daniel checked his watch. "We'd better hurry, we don't want to miss the limo."

They headed back to the inn, the sun setting as they did. It was beautiful.

As they strolled along the driveway to the inn, they saw the limo already parked outside waiting for them. Yvonne and Bailey were waiting on the porch steps and they waved as the family approached.

"You guys ready for this?" Emily asked, excited.

They nodded, and everyone got inside the limo.

As promised, Roman had installed a bubble machine for the girls to play with, and there was an ice bucket filled with alcohol-free champagne for the grown-ups. Pop music thumped as they drove, which the children loved but Emily found a little grating. She couldn't wait for the much more mature and pleasant sounds of Roman's jazz music.

They arrived at the Portland venue, which didn't even look like a concert was about to take place. Roman had managed to keep his launch party secret, and there were no signs or posters proclaiming his attendance that evening. No paparazzi stood around to take photos. Instead, it was just a group of fans lining up outside. There were more fans inside, Emily soon discovered, as they were shown through as VIPs by the security team.

The place had been decked out with couches and large floor pillows. Fabric was draped all over the walls and ceiling. It was a very relaxing environment. Everyone settled down and got comfortable. All around them, eager fans chatted with one another, exchanging excited whispers, guessing what the new album would be like.

"This is so strange," Chantelle said to Emily. "Roman's our friend but all these people are talking about him like he's super important."

Yvonne leaned in and added, wryly, "I just heard someone say they wonder what color fedora he'll be wearing tonight."

Just then the lights dimmed and the crowd erupted with applause. A moment later, Roman walked on stage. His fedora was black, matching his suit.

Chantelle giggled. "He looks funny like that," she said.

Roman's band began to strike out the first notes of the new song, and everyone started clapping along and cheering. Emily also found it strange to watch him up on stage with his swagger. Though she'd obviously known him before, she had grown more accustomed to his non-stage persona. It was quite impressive really, the way he could switch on this confident, slightly arrogant act, when it didn't really match his personality in the slightest.

The new song was great, though, and Emily bopped along with the rest of the audience. The kids were having a great time, dancing enthusiastically. Bailey's natural energy always rubbed off a little on Chantelle, making her act more goofy than normal.

Roman spotted them both in the crowd then, and waved. Chantelle waved back.

When the song ended, everyone started to cheer loudly.

"Thank you very much," Roman said, sounding for a moment like Elvis's long-lost brother. Then he pointed to Chantelle. When she looked up, he beckoned. "I'd like you to welcome a good friend of mine," he said to the crowd. "A little lady by the name of Chantelle."

Chantelle looked behind her for Emily and Daniel. When they made eye contact, Emily nodded, ushering her to go. Chantelle did, stepping up on stage carefully. The crowd clapped.

Roman whispered something in Chantelle's ear, and she nodded. Then he handed her a microphone.

Emily looked at Daniel wide-eyed. "What are they doing?" she said. "I thought he was just going to have her on stage for the fun of it. He's not expecting her to sing, is he?"

Daniel looked as bewildered as Emily felt. Yvonne was surprised as well.

"Did you know this was going to happen?" she asked.

Emily shook her head. "I don't think Chantelle did either, by the look on her face!"

The band played again, and Roman started a new song. Chantelle looked a little awkward standing next to him, swaying her hips in time to the music. But she was enjoying the beat and she relaxed as the song progressed. It helped that Roman kept singing at her, taking her attention away from the eyes that watched her from the audience.

When the chorus kicked in he nodded to her as a prompt. To Emily's delight, Chantelle sang timidly along with the backup singers. It was just a melody without words—except "doo doo doo"—but she did it perfectly. She grinned with triumph once the chorus was over.

Emily cheered, thrilled to see her up on the stage. Daniel too looked mesmerized and beyond proud. They watched and bopped along as Roman sang the second verse. Then the chorus came in again and this time, Chantelle wasn't timid at all. This time she'd found her confidence and her groove as she belted out the melody. Roman looked impressed and gave her a thumbs-up. The audience seemed delighted as well and cheered her on.

Then the chorus ended and the song went into the bridge. The lights faded, and the background instruments became more sparse, with just the drumbeat and double bass. Standing in the spotlight, Roman's solo voice filled the room. Then he looked down and nodded, and Chantelle took a step into the spotlight. She sang the counter melody perfectly, the two of them singing it while looking at each other like it was a duet that had been rehearsed a hundred times. Their voices began to swell and rise in volume, with emotion, and the backing band added to the crescendo.

The crowd was going wild. Then the stage lights flashed as the final chorus began, Chantelle taking front and center stage with her newfound confidence. Emily was stunned. She'd never seen this side of Chantelle before, nor heard this side to her voice. Usually she sounded like an angel, her voice perfectly suiting a choir. But this time she sounded like an old soul singer, like she was channeling the emotions of someone from the past. The singing lessons with Owen were paying off, clearly!

Daniel looked utterly stunned, and Emily noticed him wipe a tear away.

With the crash of symbols, the song ended, and the whole audience jumped up and down, screaming their applause.

"Chantelle, everyone!" Roman announced. He took her hand and they both bowed.

Emily clapped so hard her hands stung. Yvonne whooped loudly. Daniel was so thrilled by the whole thing he started laughing with delight.

Emily couldn't believe it. Chantelle had been given a moment in the spotlight and she had grabbed the opportunity with both hands.

It was the most amazing moment she'd ever seen—and she only prayed now that it would be the beginning of wonderful things to come.

CHAPTER TWENTY SEVEN

In the limo on the way home, everyone chatted excitedly about the amazing concert.

"I can't believe how much of a natural you were up there," Yvonne told Chantelle as she poured herself another glass of fizzy champagne.

Chantelle beamed with pride.

"I'm telling everyone when we get back to school," Bailey said. "I took a million photographs."

Emily smiled to herself, thrilled by how wonderful the evening had gone and how amazing Chantelle had really been.

Then Roman's car dropped Yvonne and Bailey off at home and proceeded on toward the Inn at Sunset Harbor. Chantelle dozed in the back seat, exhausted from all the excitement and the long day of fun.

When the car turned onto West Street, Daniel pressed the button that allowed him to communicate with the driver.

"Could you drop us off at the house next to the inn?" he asked.

"Sure," the driver confirmed.

Daniel sat back and Emily frowned at him with confusion. "We're stopping outside Trevor's?"

Daniel grinned. "Surprise."

Suddenly, it dawned on Emily what he meant. Labor Day. The work was complete.

"It's finished now?" she squealed.

Daniel nodded vigorously, looking proud as the car pulled up outside the house that was once Trevor's. Then he shook Chantelle awake.

"We're home," he said.

She stirred and looked out the window. "Trevor's?" she asked.

"It's part of our home now," Emily said, her stomach fluttering with excitement. "The renovation work is done."

Chantelle seemed to lurch awake. "It is? It's done? We can see it?"

Both Emily and Daniel nodded.

Hastily, they tumbled out of the limousine, thanking the driver, and hurried the final few steps up to the front door. Emily unlocked the door, her hands shaking with anticipation, then pushed it open.

An enormous shadow-filled space opened out before them. All the internal walls had been removed, but the staircase remained, now floating, looking grand and opulent. The floor gleamed a pristine white. Chantelle gasped.

They went inside, treading carefully as though they were walking on something fragile and precious. At the back was the open-plan kitchen and the large authentic pizza oven.

"What's upstairs?" Chantelle asked.

"The bathrooms for the restaurant," Emily explained. "And then some apartments for families."

"Can we look?"

Emily nodded yes. They all went up the stairs. The new restrooms were very plush, exactly the sort of high-end rooms that Emily had wanted. Better, even, than her imagination had conjured.

Down the hall they came to the new apartment doors. Emily was excited to look inside, knowing that the architects had had to completely redesign the layout in order to give as many of them as possible ocean views. Seeing all the doors lined up this way was like looking at a surrealist picture. She knew behind some there would be stairs leading up, while others would open straight into a living space, and others still would begin with a winding corridor. The place was like a labyrinth and it just added to the joy of it. She thought Roy would be very proud of the maze-like design.

Chantelle opened the first door and they saw an ascending staircase. The smell of fresh paint wafted out. They climbed the stairs, the new carpet soft beneath their feet, and the room opened out before them. It was a gorgeous space, compact but with all the essentials. Off the main room, which contained a kitchenette, was a bathroom, a master bedroom, and two smaller rooms with bunk beds. But the real star attractions were the enormous windows with their ocean view.

"This is amazing!" Chantelle cried, twirling in circles. Her earlier tiredness seemed to have disappeared entirely in all the excitement.

"Let's look at the others," Emily cried.

They hurried downstairs and went into the next apartment. This door opened straight into the living area, with the same shaped living room and kitchenette, the ocean view windows sitting directly beneath the room above. But this apartment was more interesting as it was set over two floors. The wooden staircase led up to a master bedroom and two smaller rooms that had attic feels. It was very homely.

"I like this one even better!" Chantelle exclaimed.

Emily got the distinct impression she would say that about every one of the apartments they looked inside.

In the next suite there was a staircase that led them, this time, to the bedrooms and bathroom first. A further staircase took them into what Emily realized must be the attic, and here, to her surprise, was the main living area with French doors that opened out onto the widow's walk. There was a bistro table outside with chairs.

Emily gasped as she realized something. This third room was utilizing the outside widow's walk, which meant the people who rented it would still get ocean views. The Erik & Sons brothers must have moved the puzzle pieces around to make sure they got the view from all the rooms, just like Emily wanted.

Filled with awe, they rushed through the rest of the apartments, each one unique, and each one with an ocean view cleverly manipulated into the space. Emily was stunned. The place was like a rabbit warren, all the rooms designed to sit on top of one another so that no single one would be without the amazing view.

"Did you know about this?" she asked Daniel.

He smiled. "I might've had a bit of a hand in the redesigning."

Emily threw her arms around him, overjoyed. Daniel held her tightly. Then he jerked away.

"She kicked me!" he laughed. "Baby Charlotte. I felt her."

Emily gasped. Chantelle ran over from the window she'd been gazing out of. Everyone pressed a hand to Emily's stomach and waited with bated breath.

Then Emily felt it. Charlotte. A kick. A hello.

"Hello, little one," she said.

EPILOGUE

Emily listened to the sound of Chantelle and Daniel playing in the living room. She herself was sitting in her office, at the desk that had once belonged to her father. Amongst the mail she had collected that morning, she'd noticed one in her father's handwriting and had stashed it away, wanting to read it quietly and in privacy once the hecticness of the day was over.

She leaned back in the chair and took a breath, then opened the letter. Her father's scrawling handwriting filled her with a sense of nostalgia. She was sure she could smell the clock grease on the paper mixing with the metallic odor of cogs. She breathed it in, comforted, as if her father were here in the room.

When she'd first seen it this morning, she'd wondered whether the first letter Roy had sent would contain the diary entries he'd told her about, the ones that explained every detail he could remember related to every photograph he had of her. The enormous scrapbook he'd told her he would make. But no, this was an ordinary letter addressed to her directly.

Emily Jane,

We just finished speaking on the telephone. As a father, hearing my daughter cry is the most painful sound in the world. But I need you to know how necessary and important it is to do so, to be in touch with your emotions. Things cannot be good all the time. Flowers cannot always bloom. In life there is sadness, there is pain. And there must be. Because through these trials there is triumph, growth, and learning. Without the winter, we would never appreciate the sun.

My darling, I love you.

Dad

Emily couldn't help herself from crying. But they weren't tears of grief, they were tears of gratitude. Of joy, even. Her life was richer than some people's would ever be, despite the hardships. Her father's letter was the perfect reminder. They were words to live by. She would frame it to keep it safe forevermore. Then, perhaps one day she and Chantelle would bury it in a time capsule. The thought made her smile to herself.

She left her office and stood in the corridor. The inn had grown increasingly quiet over the last few weeks. Now that Labor Day weekend was over, along with summer, they would have a quieter spell. And with more staff, things felt less chaotic.

She went toward the living room but then paused, not quite ready to share Roy's letter with anyone. She wanted to keep it to herself for a while, to let his words be spoken just for her. So instead, she went softly upstairs.

Something seemed to be drawing her toward Baby Charlotte's room, and she let the sensation guide her along the hall and inside. The room had been fixed up now, since Chantelle's meltdown, and it had been freshly painted in the most delicate creamy pink color. It looked gorgeous and comfortable.

Emily sat in the nursing chair and looked about her, envisioning the future when she would be here, cradling a newborn, feeding her and caring for her. A tingle of excitement spread throughout her entire body.

As the moon rose, making shadows lengthen across the floor, Emily noticed that one of the boxes of toys she'd stored in the attic when she first moved in was sitting in the middle of the floor. She wondered whether Daniel had brought it down. She certainly hadn't.

She went and crouched beside it, opening up the lid. The first thing she saw inside was a rag doll that had belonged to Charlotte, with rosy circles stitched onto its cheeks and stringy red hair. It was still in good condition despite having been locked away in her sister's old room for decades.

She stroked her fingers through the doll's hair of string. Then she stood and placed the doll delicately into the crib.

She stepped back to take in the sight. It seemed only fitting that Baby Charlotte's first toy would be one that had belonged to the aunt she was named for.

As she looked around at the nursery, growing dimmer in the darkening night, she sighed with contentment. The cycle of life was turning.

Returning downstairs to her family, Emily found that they had moved onto the porch to watch the beautiful starry sky. She waltzed toward them, filled to the brim with love. Daniel looked up as she approached, his eyes filled with delight at her presence. He reached for her and she folded against him.

Just then, she heard the sound of his phone ringing. She shuffled off his lap so he could fish his phone out of his pocket.

"It's the real estate agent calling me back," he said.

Emily felt a sudden jolt of excitement race through her. Chantelle turned and watched. She looked as nervous as Emily felt as they watched Daniel take the call.

He spoke for a moment, recounting that they were inquiring about the island, then covered the receiver.

"It's still for sale," he told Chantelle and Emily. "The island."

Chantelle grabbed Emily's hand.

"Are we putting in an offer?" Daniel asked Emily. "Are we really doing this?"

Her nerves fluttering, Emily's eyes fell to the telescope clutched in Chantelle's hand. The word Sunset Island was clearly visible. All the signs were there. And hadn't she told Amy that sometimes you had to take a leap of faith in life? To jump into things with both feet? Hadn't she told her father he had to live his final months to the fullest, to have as many experiences as possible?

She grinned, the answer forming so perfectly and clearly in her mind.

"Yes," she said, firmly, as confident as she could be that this was the right thing to do. "Yes, we really are."

NOW AVAILABLE!

FOR YOU, FOREVER
(The Inn at Sunset Harbor—Book 6)

Sophie Love's ability to impart magic to her readers is exquisitely wrought in powerfully evocative phrases and descriptions....This is the perfect romance or beach read, with a difference: its enthusiasm and beautiful descriptions offer an unexpected attention to the complexity of not just evolving love, but evolving psyches. It's a delightful recommendation for romance readers looking for a touch more complexity from their romance reads."
--*Midwest Book Review* (Diane Donovan re *For Now and Forever*)

FOR YOU, FOREVER is book #7 in the #1 bestselling romance series THE INN AT SUNSET HARBOR, which begins with For Now and Forever (book #1).

Fall has arrived in Sunset Harbor, and as the town clears out, Emily Mitchell enters her second trimester. Their new rooms at Trevor's house open for their first guests, while their new spa and restaurant open for business. All the while, they pursue their bid on the island, hoping to add yet another dimension to their life at Sunset Harbor.

Amy insists on throwing Emily a layette in New York City, and Emily returns to her old home, in shock at how much she has changed—and at the unwanted guests who show up. She is mortified to learn that there will be a new resident of Sunset Harbor—a NYC developer who will open a rival inn—and destroy Emily's business.

Chantelle goes back to school, but her new grade is an unpleasant surprise, and as things don't work out, the drama puts her into a tailspin.

Roy is getting sicker, and as the weather turns cold, he invites them all to a getaway in his home in Greece, and Emily, although worried for her growing baby, cannot refuse. It is a trip that will change all of them forever, culminating in a Thanksgiving none of them will forget.

FOR YOU, FOREVER is book #7 in a dazzling new romance series that will make you laugh, cry, keep you turning pages late into the night—and make you fall in love with romance all over again.

Book #8 will be available soon. Sophie's new romance series, LOVE LIKE THIS, is now also available!

"A very well written novel, describing the struggle of a woman (Emily) to find her true identity. The author did an amazing job with the creation of the characters and her description of the environment. The romance is there, but not overdosed. Kudos to the author for this amazing start of a series that promises to be very entertaining."
--*Books and Movies Reviews*, Roberto Mattos (re *For Now and Forever*)

Sophie Love

#1 bestselling author Sophie Love is author of the romantic comedy series THE INN AT SUNSET HARBOR, which includes seven books (and counting), and which begins with FOR NOW AND FOREVER (THE INN AT SUNSET HARBOR—BOOK 1).

Sophie Love is also the author of the debut romantic comedy series, THE ROMANCE CHRONICLES, which begins with LOVE LIKE THIS (THE ROMANCE CHRONICLES—BOOK 1).

Sophie would love to hear from you, so please visit www.sophieloveauthor.com to email her, to join the mailing list, to receive free ebooks, to hear the latest news, and to stay in touch!

BOOKS BY SOPHIE LOVE

THE INN AT SUNSET HARBOR
FOR NOW AND FOREVER (Book #1)
FOREVER AND FOR ALWAYS (Book #2)
FOREVER, WITH YOU (Book #3)
IF ONLY FOREVER (Book #4)
FOREVER AND A DAY (Book #5)
FOREVER, PLUS ONE (Book #6)
FOR YOU, FOREVER (Book #7)

THE ROMANCE CHRONICLES
LOVE LIKE THIS (Book #1)
LOVE LIKE THAT (Book #2)

Made in the USA
Middletown, DE
30 September 2019